Tommy Turner's
Tremendous Travels

Tommy Turner's
` Tremendous Travels

Ali Seegar

Illustrations by Patrick Hawkins

Edited by Marlo Garnsworthy

A. K. Kingsbury
2016

First printing: 2016

ISBN 978-99959-965-0-5

A. K. Kingsbury
32 Avenue Berchem
L-1231, Howald, Luxembourg

www.tommy-turner.com

Ordering information:
Special discounts are available on quantity purchases by corporations, associations, educators, trade bookstores and wholesalers.

Please contact the publisher at the address above or email:
hello@tommy-turner.com

Illustrations by Patrick Hawkins: www.patrickhawkins.co.uk

Dedication

For Meriel, Gabriel, Fred and Tommy
in memory of Em.

✎ Chapter 1 ✎

In Which We Meet Tommy

'Phazanggggg,' cried Tommy as he leapt onto his bike and sped off down the driveway of his new house in Parsons Court.

A tingle of excitement bubbled inside him, like a fizzy drink about to explode. It ran down his legs and arms and buzzed about his head as he gathered speed at the bottom of the drive. It made his skin tingle and his heart pound, and all of a sudden, the sky looked bluer than it had for many weeks. On the very last afternoon of the summer holiday, Tommy could remember what it was like to feel happy.

He had not felt this way for at least seven weeks. In fact, he had felt miserable. Just like the time he had accidentally spilt orange squash over his dad's brand-new laptop and found himself grounded for three weeks without any pocket money. In fact, Tommy had felt miserable ever since his parents had sat him down and told him they were moving house. Away from his friends, his school, and the home he had lived in for the whole of his twelve-and-a-half years.

These days, he used words he had heard his dad say when he accidentally hit his thumb with a hammer or reversed his car into the dustbin. Tommy had got to quite like using them; they made him feel a whole lot better.

Like the word he had said to himself when his parents told him about his new school.

They had been in the middle of eating his favourite supper of bangers and mash, and Tommy had just stuck a huge forkful of buttery potato into his mouth, when his mum leant forward and grinned at him. It was a strange, unnatural grin. The sort of grin you might expect to see on a politician, and a chill trickled down his back. There was only one thing it could mean. Trouble. Normally, his mum only smiled at really important people, like the bank manager and his dad's boss. And his six-year-younger sister, Sally.

'Tommy, darling,' said his mum, a little too brightly. This worried him even more. She never said 'darling' to him.

She paused for a moment and then gave a bright laugh. Tommy gulped down his mash in anticipation.

'Tommy, we have the most exciting news to tell you. Haven't we, Gordon?' She nudged Tommy's dad, who appeared from behind the newspaper he was absorbed in.

'Hurrumph,' he said, spearing a large piece of sausage onto his fork before returning to his reading. 'You tell him. You're better at it than me.'

'Oh, Tommy,' trilled his mum as she cut up some dainty portions of sausage to feed to Sally, 'you'll never guess in a million years, so I'll tell you straight out. We—your father and I, that is—have found you the most amazing, wonderful new school. High Brooms, it's called. High Brooms.' She repeated the name slowly for added effect. 'The very best boarding school in the—'

'BOARDING SCHOOL!' exclaimed Tommy. (This was when he muttered the word to himself).

'Yes, yes, but you, my darling, will be one of the dayboys.' His mum shoved a piece of sausage into Sally's mouth, which was beaming from ear to ear at the look of horror etched on Tommy's face. Nothing delighted her more than to see her brother looking miserable.

'But what about me staying at Forrester? What about Digby—and the gang—and what about the football team?' A queasy gurgle galloped around Tommy's stomach. He pushed his food away, too anxious to eat another mouthful. 'I was going to be made captain this year,' he said quietly.

'Ah well, there's a slight problem there,' his dad replied briskly, folding up his paper and clearing his throat. 'Hurrumph. Go on, Pernilla. Don't keep the boy waiting.'

Tommy glanced across at his dad's fat, rosy face then back at his mum's brightly coloured one. They both beamed at him as though he had just won the lottery.

'What problem?' he gulped, fighting back the lump that was welling up in his throat.

'Well, Tommy darling, the house we've bought is rather—'

'HOUSE!' cried Tommy.

'Don't yell, Tommy dear. High Broom boys certainly do not yell. Now, where were we? Oh yes. The fact of the matter is that the house is rather far from here, and it'll be a bit difficult to—well, you know—travel the distance. But I'm sure you will make lots of new friends. And the right sort of friends at that. Some of the parents of High Brooms are terribly important diplomats. Just think of the parties we—umm—you'll be invited to. It will be simply marvellous, won't it, Gordon.'

His dad nodded his agreement and rubbed his podgy hands together.

Tommy felt as though a boa constrictor had suddenly shot up the chair leg and wrapped itself around his ribs. The mash he had just swallowed was threatening to show itself again. But the only thing he said was, 'What about Digby?'

Digby was his best friend and fellow adventurer. They had met on the very first day of primary school and remained best friends for the last eight years. There was nothing Tommy had done without Digby as his sidekick, and they had stood side by side through thick and thin, all the years they had known each other. It looked as though all this would now end.

'Digby can come and stay with you at half term.' His mum's voice broke into Tommy's thoughts. 'Now, no more whatabouts. Your father has been given the most wonderful opportunity with a very important company and we're moving in four weeks' time, whether you like it or not.'

*

The new house at Parsons Court looked like a large brick box. An identical brick box to the other seven brick boxes in this (according to the estate agent) exclusive cul-de-sac. Tommy hated his tiny square bedroom; it was half the size of his old one and still smelled of paint. And it was just not fair that Sally's room was larger than his, even though she was six years younger. But then everything was Sally. Sally and her dancing. Sally and her horse riding. Sally and her specialness. Sally, Sally, Sally. He might as well not exist as long as his brat of a sister had all she needed.

And then there was High Brooms.

Last week, his mum had taken him shopping for his new uniform. Grey with purple trim. As the shop assistant finished knotting his tie, Tommy had squeezed his eyes tight and prayed with all his might that the next day his parents would receive a letter from the school, regretting that 'unfortunately, we will not be able to offer Tommy a place after all.'

Then he had opened his eyes again and stared in horror at his unfamiliar reflection in the changing room mirror.

His dark hair, which usually sprouted forth in wild clumps like he had declared war on it, was pasted to his head like a skullcap with the ton of gel his mum had smeared over it that morning. His gangly legs, which seemed to have grown four inches longer this summer, were sticking out of a horrid pair of old-fashioned trousers, and the ensemble was topped with an equally nasty blazer to match. His face was turning an alarming shade of purple (a result of the assistant's over-zealous tightening of his tie). Only his denim-blue eyes and a smattering of freckles across his broad nose gave any hint to the fact it was he.

'Oh, don't you look lovely?' his mum said. Tommy scowled back at her.

'A right little gentleman,' agreed the assistant enthusiastically.

'Look, Sally, doesn't your brother look handsome?' Sally, who was clutching a newly-bought doll, nodded. 'He will never be beautiful like you, my little angel,' continued his mum in her high-pitched screech, 'but at least he will be presentable.'

The long-wished-for letter never arrived, but instead, the first day of term crept nearer and nearer until finally it was tomorrow.

Throughout the holidays, Tommy's heart had felt as grey and cloudy as the endless rain-lashed days. He had spent most of his spare time sitting in his tiny square bedroom, watching the rain cascade down the window and daydreaming about the fun he could be having if Digby and the gang were with him.

But today, on the very last day of the holidays, as Tommy sat huddled on his bedroom windowsill, the sun peeked out from between the dark rain clouds and smiled down on him, as if to say, 'Cheer up, it ain't so bad.' He felt the warmth of its rays hitting his left cheek, which was squashed against the windowpane, and it made him smile. His tummy (which had been churning about like a trapped eel at the thought of putting on his grey and purple uniform the next time he woke up) gave a last loud, squelchy rumble.

Before he knew it, Tommy had jumped off the windowsill, narrowly avoiding the pile of comics thrown in a heap by his bed. *I've had enough of feeling miserable,* he thought, hurrying towards the door. *If I can't go on an adventure with Digby, then I'll find one of my own,* he vowed, tearing down the stairs two at a time.

Hurray, said his old self, who had been hidden away for far too long. He sprinted around the corner, grabbed his bike and, with one giant bound, leapt onto it.

'Phazanggggg,' he cried triumphantly, speeding off down the driveway of his new house.

He streaked past Mr Brown, who spun around in such a fright that he tripped right over his Doberman, Fred. He pelted past the postman, who was on a late delivery. He charged round the cul-de-sac corner, slowing only to let Mrs Collins jump onto the pavement, and dashed down Evergreen Hill. He was not sure where he was going or what he would do when he got there, but right now it did not matter in the slightest.

❧ Chapter 2 ❧

A Box Full of What?

On the other side of town, as Tommy was jumping off his windowsill, Nicolas Petrovsky was standing halfway up a rickety stepladder, down below in the murky depths of his toy store stockroom. He was staring at a large cardboard box. It was as normal a cardboard box as a cardboard box could be, except—and that was the weirdest thing—he could not remember seeing it before, let alone putting it there.

He climbed another rung on the ladder for a closer look and noticed a strange scent drifting from the package. It was such a familiar smell, and yet, try as he might, he could not place it. He sniffed again. Then again, deeper, trying to soak the scent into his body. What could it be? He knew he knew it, but—

The sweet, spicy aroma filled his lungs. and long-forgotten memories flooded through him.

The smell of his grandmother's *kulich* cake. *BANG*—the oven door snapping closed behind her as she carried it steaming to the table. 'Don't touch, *rebenok*, or you'll burn your fingers.'

WHOOOOSH.

Now he was nine years old, on the huge ship that had carried them here. Fish stench and sea-salt tang. Reeking wet rope. Promenading parasol-ladies' perfume. Horns blowing and shouts of 'Land!' The tight grip of his father's giant hand around his own miniature copy. Days past. Another world—his childhood Russia. A life truly different from the one he had become a man in, impossible to compare.

Ohhh, but that smell!

He jerked back to the present, swaying slightly as his mind refocused. Carefully, he reached for the box and grabbed one of the edges with his fingertips. The box inched towards him, enabling him to get a firmer grip, and he pulled again until it was almost on top of his head. It was not as heavy as he had imagined, just big and bulky, and the dust irritated his nose and mouth.

Mr Petrovsky manoeuvred the box until it was resting on his chest. Then he slowly descended the rungs.

At the foot of the ladder he let the box slide to the floor and, with a great sigh, sat upon it. *I'm too old for this malarkey*, he thought, and the box sagged as if in agreement.

When at last his heart rate had steadied, Mr Petrovsky got up from his seat, brushing off his trousers as he did so, and pulled another large box towards him in order to sit again. Now he could properly examine his find.

As he had thought, the box was very old. Almost rotten. The tape, which had done its best over the years to keep the contents secret, had become sticky with age and left a gooey mess on his fingers when he touched it.

Reaching into his trouser pocket, Mr Petrovsky pulled out the small silver penknife he always carried with him and sliced open the tape. As he did, the unforgettable, indistinguishable scent drifted once again to his nostrils. *What on earth is that smell?* he mused. It was as though all the most wonderful odours he had ever smelt in his life had blended together and transformed into a majestic perfume.

Gingerly, he opened the cardboard flaps and peered inside. Disappointment flooded over him at his discovery. There were no toys. No tricks or magic. No models or games. Just a pile of clothes. T-shirts to be more exact.

T-shirts! Never in his life had he ordered clothes for the shop. Why would he when there were already enough clothing stores in town? And T-shirts. He hated T-shirts, thought they were one of the main reasons people looked so untailored and casual these days. T-shirts and baseball caps. He would never be seen dead in a T-shirt, or a baseball cap for that matter. A crisply ironed shirt, fresh and clean each morning, was his standard uniform. And proud of it he was, too.

But still, they were something to sell in the shop. And, as he had somehow received them free of charge, he could make a very nice profit. In fact, it would be a good test. If they sold well, maybe he would add a small range of clothing to his stock. He chuckled to himself, *Hey ho, maybe this is a good day after all. A fine catch. The start of a whole new business venture.*

He reached in and took the top T-shirt from the box, its cellophane wrapper crackling as he did so. This one was orange, but there were many different colours: blue, red, purple, pink. A rainbow of colours.

He slit the seal of the package with his knife, withdrew the shirt, and unfolded it.

What a wonderful surprise he got. Printed on the front was the word 'MAGIC!' in big, glittery letters. They shimmered even in the dimly-lit stockroom. Translucent, shimmering water, but at the same time bright, dazzling and boldly colourful. The word said 'MAGIC!' and it looked magic, too. And the fabric. That was something else. Mr Petrovsky had never in his seventy-three years felt such fabric. It was as soft as kitten fur. And warm, as though it wanted to envelop him. Draw him into its magical secrets.

He lifted the shirt to his face, so he could feel the softness against his skin. As he did, the sweet aroma of his grandmother's *kulich* cake flooded the air around him.

*

A few moments later, Nicolas Petrovsky emerged from the top of the stockroom stairs, puffing and wheezing like a rusty locomotive. He dragged the bulky cardboard box up the last few steps and onto the shop floor. The bright spotlights bore into his eyes, and he blinked back tears as they adjusted to the bright shop lighting. Outside the rain had started to lash down once again, and the sound of rush-hour cars whooshing through the puddles filled his ears. Summer was going. The evenings were closing in earlier each week. Soon he would be getting ready for Halloween.

He loved this shop, his family's shop. He had helped out in it when he was twelve, worked in it since he was sixteen, and owned it for the last thirty-four years. His father would have been proud of him, though maybe slightly miffed by some of the changes his son had made over the years.

Still, it was pretty much the same as he remembered from his childhood, when his father had transformed it into Petrovsky's Toy Store.

Stretching up to relieve some knots pinging between his shoulder blades, Mr Petrovsky looked around for a prominent position in which to display the hoard of T-shirts. He settled in the end for a small window display and a large basket just inside the entrance.

He tried not to think of the tiredness creaking through his bones, but instead pushed the box over to the front of the store and set to work on the changes, humming a melodic tune as he worked.

He had almost emptied the box—his mind already focused on how welcoming his slippers would be once he got back home—when he noticed an unwrapped T-shirt hidden within the armful he had just scooped up. He pulled it out of the bundle, intending to throw it amongst the rubbish he had already accumulated. Without warning, an explosion of energy shot through his fingertips. It raced up his arms, surged into his shoulders, tumbled through his tummy and leapt down his legs, making him cry out with joy. His body tingled with energy; its obstinate aches already a distant memory. His mind felt as crisp as a freshly starched sheet.

The extraordinarily ordinary T-shirt lay limply in his hands. Its plainness, so unlike the other garments in the box, was as uninspiring as its muddy grey colour, and yet the aura radiating from it was unearthly. Supernatural, as if it were a sacred cloth fallen from heaven. Mr Petrovsky felt humbled and ashamed to be even holding it yet invincible and freshly born.

He brought the cloth up to his cheek, enveloping his face in its soft folds. There it was again. How strange. The smell of his grandmother's *kulich* cake.

Tommy Turner's Tremendous Travels

ᔰ Chapter 3 ᔱ

High Brooms

Friday afternoon had at long last arrived. In the school playground of High Brooms, Tommy was waiting, as usual, for his mum. All around him, a ghostly silence replaced the usual banter and chaos of break-times. His Year Eight classmates were up in their dormitory doing homework, and the other dayboys had long since departed, so—apart from himself and an ant army marching methodically back and forth along the brick path—all was quiet. The only other detectable movement was Mr Jenkins' head appearing from time to time at the staffroom window to check if Tommy was still there.

He watched the line of ants struggling to bring a large crumb back to their nest, then mooched over to the old wooden gate that marked the school boundary. He climbed the rungs, the gate protesting at his weight. At the top he sat and thought about his miserable life.

The first two weeks at High Brooms had been worse than he had ever imagined possible. Tommy felt as though he must be invisible or, at the very least, riddled with the plague. He wanted to yell at the top of his lungs, 'I'm here, too!' as the other boys kept a wide berth and huddled together in their newly formed gangs, swapping jokes and sharing music. It was not his fault he was the only dayboy in his year. It was not fair he had to stay in the Dayboy's Room while the other boys went up to their dorms. He was sick of sitting at the bottom of the stairs and listening to the fun and laughter drifting along the corridor. Why had his stupid dad gotten his stupid job? Why did he have to come to this stupid, snobby, stuck-up school? A pang of jealousy sliced through his chest as he remembered Digby and his old gang would be off to football training right now. He should be there too; perhaps he would even be playing in the County Under 16s by now; after all, that guy had come to their football match last June and had picked him to come and try out. But then his mum had smiled that sickly smile at him and told him his whole world was ending.

He jumped off the gate into the street and kicked a couple of stones in frustration. Where was his mum anyway? She was never normally this late. Maybe she had forgotten him.

'No one here to get you yet, Turner?' Mr Jenkins called from the staffroom window. Tommy looked round at his form master and shook his head.

'Well, get back inside the gates. You know the rules.' Mr Jenkins' head disappeared back to his marking.

Tommy stuck his foot onto the second rung, ready to hoist himself over the gate, when he felt his shirt being tugged from behind.

'Still here, worm brains?' a low voice growled in his ear. 'You know the rules. Dayboys ain't welcome after four-thirty, and d'you know what time it is?'

Tommy's stomach lurched towards his legs, which had turned into two tubes of cooked macaroni. He felt himself being yanked off the gate and spun around to face his captors. Staring at him with mean, squinty eyes stood Shaun Higgins, while his twin brother, Stu, leered over his shoulder.

Blimey, the Higgins Twins! High Brooms' biggest bullies. Their favourite pastimes, he had heard, were beating up smaller kids and smoking behind the bike shed. Even the teachers were terrified of them.

'I said, d'you know what time it is?' repeated Shaun, poking him hard in the chest.

Tommy's words stuck in his throat. 'No—sorry—I haven't —'

'Haven't what, eh? Haven't got a watch? Haven't got a clue?' Shaun smirked, nudging Stu in the ribs to egg him on.

'That's alright, isn't it, bruv,' sneered Stu, moving a little closer. 'We don't need a watch today. It's something else we want.'

Tommy's mind whirled round and round like a mouse spinning a wheel. His mouth felt dry with fear. Could he escape? Not a chance; he was trapped between the gate and the two louts. Should he fight them? If he did, he would, without a doubt, be pulp in two seconds. Where was Mr Jenkins when he really needed him?

'I was thinking, see, how you live at home,' said Shaun. 'Your folks must have plenty of dosh. And I'm a bit skint at the mo. Seem to have spent all mine. So, I thought you could give me some of yours.'

'I don't have any on me, honestly,' Tommy replied, hoping his face would not betray the lie he had just told. Most of his pocket money he had been saving for the past few months was buried away in his secret coat pocket.

'Don't have any, eh? Well, I'm not sure I believe you. Why don't Stu here have a check?'

Tommy backed towards the gate, wishing he could dissolve into the pavement beneath him. Stu grabbed his shirt collar. He leaned forward, his breath hot and cloying on Tommy's face.

'So, where'd you like me to start?' he sneered.

A rush of anger shot through Tommy's body, crushing the fear that had overwhelmed him seconds before. There was no way he was going to let these thugs steal his money. He would fight them tooth and nail before they got a penny. Adrenaline pumped and banged through his head. Stu swung back his arm, ready to take aim, ready to strike. Tommy felt his body tense, his fists clenching in response.

The sound of a distant car horn cut into his concentration. Then again, nearer, honking them back to reality. His mum drew up, flinging the passenger door wide open.

Panic spread over the two brothers' faces, and Stu quickly released his grip on Tommy. He patted Tommy on the back as if to show they had just been having a quiet little chat and grunted at Shaun to leave. As they turned to go, Shaun grasped Tommy's arm, his tight grip burning into Tommy's flesh.

'Bailed out by Mumsy this time, but she won't be here on Monday. You've the weekend to sort something out.' Then, with a nod at Stu, the two brothers slunk off down the road.

'In. Now.'

Tommy bent down to get his coat and hefty school bag. He was trembling with a mixture of fear, rage and indignation.

'Hurry up! We haven't got all day,' snorted his mum, her shiny, red lips quivering with impatience. Sally sat primly in the back, her new pink ballet tutu wafting around her legs.

Tommy climbed in and tried to calm his breathing. He felt sick at the thought of what Monday would bring. Shaun would certainly seek him out and demand some money. Perhaps he could fake a stomach-ache or flu and not go to school. At least, he had the weekend to think of something.

His mum looked at him and smiled her sickly smile. 'Nice to see you are making friends at last, Thomas.'

The door closed, and off she screeched, rubber burning, while Tommy glanced back to see his new school receding into the distance.

High Brooms was a large Victorian red brick building full of long, winding corridors and towering ceilings. The present headmaster, Mr Hargreeves, had himself been a pupil there many years ago. Now that he ruled over the school, 'expulsion' was his favourite word, and he did not hesitate to use it. Tommy looked through the car window with a pang of longing. If only Digby were there with him. If only he had some friends to laugh with. But how could it ever be possible if no one would even speak to him?

The teachers were also against him, it seemed. Mr Jenkins, their form teacher, was forever sneaking up behind him and threatening to whack him with a ruler. But Tommy could not help it if he was a daydreamer. He did not mean to think about other things. It just happened without him realising. The other day, he had been sitting in maths, staring out of the classroom window, while Mr Philips droned on and on about multiplication. It was not that Tommy hated maths; he just found it boring. Outside in the far distance, he could see Year Ten playing football: Mr Adams blowing his whistle and one of the boys rolling on the ground clutching his knee.

Turner! GOOOAAAAALLLL!!!!

He imagined himself there, at Wembley, the final minute of the FA Cup. Crowds cheering as the magical foot of Tommy Turner saved the match. He would be lifted high by his teammates and carried around the pitch. Man of the Match. Cameras flashing. Reporters clambering to get the best interview. And Tommy. The Hero. He would be made captain, invited to play in the World Cup.

ENGLAND WOULD BE SAVED.

'— and what do you think the answer is, Turner?'

Tommy looked in panic at Mr Philips, who was staring meanly at him. Now everyone in the classroom was staring at him. Why was his brain filling with mush instead of answers?

'I'm not sure, sir,' he muttered, feeling his ears turn red hot.

'Well, what do you think the question is?' said Mr Philips, with growing impatience.

'I'm not sure, sir,' Tommy said, even more quietly. The room was as still as a morgue, the buzz of the overhead lights breaking the heavy silence.

'Not sure, eh? Well, what are you sure of, Turner?' snarled Mr Philips.

The other boys sniggered.

'Umm—'

'Oh, don't bother answering. It clearly isn't worth trying to teach you anything, but I will deal with you after class. Now, who does know the answer?'

Several hands shot up as Mr Philips continued the lesson.

'Nice one, Turner,' whispered Simon Gillett, leaning over his desk. 'You've really got it coming.'

And he had.

First, Mr Philips had given him a lecture about laziness and then a punishment: 'I shall pay attention in class and correctly answer the questions' written out two hundred times, to be completed and handed in by the following morning.

✍ Chapter 4 ✍

A Gift Is Given

Tommy patted his coat pocket to check his money was still safe and felt his stomach knot at the memory of Stu's face so close to his. But it was the weekend. They were on their way to the shopping centre, and so he decided to push the events to the back of his mind. For the time being, at least.

The car whooshed past the brightly lit shops, stopping now and then in the early evening traffic. It had started raining once again, and Tommy looked out at the multitude of brightly coloured umbrellas marching purposefully homeward in time for supper.

His thoughts were broken by Sally yelling directly into his ear, 'STOP THE CAR! I want to go there.' She pointed to an old corner shop, and Tommy swung his head round just in time to see the large gold letters of 'Petrovsky's Toy Store' disappear out of sight.

'We're off to the Blooms, my pet,' said his mum in a jovial, please-do-not-make-a-to-do kind of way.

'I don't want to go to the Blooms. I want to go there. NOW,' ordered Sally, starting to turn crimson with anger. 'You said you would buy me a present, and I want a present from THAT SHOP!'

Tommy sucked in his breath and waited for the screaming to start.

'Okay, okay, my precious one. We don't want our little princess getting upset now, do we? Of course, we can go there if you say so, Sally.' Their mum just managed to indicate, slam on the brakes and turn into the High Street carpark before the scene turned nasty. The driver behind blew his horn, and several people scurried out of the way. Sally looked delighted with herself.

*

The doorbell clanged as they entered. It was one of those large, old-fashioned brass bells that hang just above the door, with a mechanism to trigger the clanger. It resounded satisfyingly throughout the shop.

Tommy stared wide-eyed at the treasure trove of goodies stacked high on every shelf.

'Get in, get in,' said his mum, pushing him from behind. 'We'll all get soaked if you just stand there gawping.' Tommy stepped to one side as Sally rushed past him, leaving dirty wet footprints on the floor.

An old man appeared from behind the counter and, coming to the door, greeted them warmly.

'Come in, come in. Welcome to Petrovsky's Toy Store.' His dark, rich voice still hinted of his childhood roots. 'Let me take your umbrella and give you a chance to—'

He halted in his tracks, staring at Tommy with his piercing blue eyes.

'O *moj bog*, my God,' he whispered, reverting to his mother tongue. A dark shadow passed across his face as if he had just seen a ghost. '*Eto ne mozhet byt*. It can't be.'

'I want a toy,' Sally said rudely and stamped her foot on the floor for emphasis.

The old man snapped back to reality and turned to look at the petulant face before him.

'Well, you've certainly come to the right place,' said Mr Petrovsky, for of course it was he.

'I'm going to look around with Sally,' said Tommy's mum, turning to him. 'Do not touch a single thing. If anything gets broken, it will come straight out of your pocket money.' She led Sally away, pointing towards a display of My Little Pony merchandise.

Mr Petrovsky turned back to Tommy, who was still hovering by the front door.

'I've seen you before, haven't I?'

'No, sir,' replied Tommy hesitantly. He was rather afraid of this tall, white-haired man stooping towards him. 'At least, I don't think so. You see, we're new to the neighbourhood.'

'Ah, you're new here. And what should I call you?'

'I'm Tommy. Tommy Turner.'

'Tommy, eh? That's a fine name. Sorry to stare, but you just look so familiar, that's all. Well, how do you do, Tommy Turner? I am Nicolas Petrovsky and, come to think of it, this is my shop.' His laugh spread up into his twinkling eyes. 'Come and look around. I don't think it will be you who breaks anything,' he added, glancing in Sally's direction. Tommy grinned and nodded his agreement. Perhaps Mr Petrovsky was not so scary after all.

There were so many amazing things to see that Tommy did not know where to start. Mr Petrovsky led him around the store, pointing out various displays.

'Do you like model making?' he asked, showing Tommy some large boxes stacked in one corner. 'Some new aeroplane kits came in yesterday. Or what about magic?' Mr Petrovsky lowered his voice. 'Do you like playing tricks?'

His eyes sparkled again as he led Tommy towards a stand full of small tricks. Bags of pepper sweets, itching powder and plastic dog pooh could be Tommy's in exchange for just a handful of coins. His hands twitched at the thought of Sally swallowing a greedy handful of the sweets. Eventually, he turned to Mr Petrovsky.

'Do you have anything about space and Mars and the other planets and things?'

'So, you like space, do you?'

Tommy hesitated. Could he trust this old man with his secrets? He glanced around to see if his mum and Sally were nearby, then said quietly, 'I want to be an astronaut when I'm older. I want to travel the whole solar system and discover new planets that will be named after me. I want to feel what it's like to float weightlessly in space and eat dehydrated ice cream for supper every day!'

'An ice cream-loving astronaut, eh?' Mr Petrovsky chuckled.
'Well, that's if I don't get to play for England.'
'And a world-famous footballer. I'm truly glad to hear you've set
your goals high. Be true to your dreams, Tommy, for you never know
where they may take you.' Mr Petrovsky looked round. 'Now, let me
see. I do believe I have a space kit left, and I seem to remember it
having your name on it!'

Five minutes later, Tommy was watching Mr Petrovsky wrap up
his newly brought Space Station Kit. It had cost most of his pocket
money and was worth every single penny—not just for the kit itself,
but also the look on his mum's face when she came around the corner
as Mr Petrovsky was popping it into a huge brown paper bag.
'What a wonderful choice your boy has made.' The old man
smiled at her. 'Hours of entertainment and very informative, too.'
'But—' his mum started.
'And what a fine, intelligent boy you have, Mrs Turner,'
continued Mr Petrovsky, his voice rising above hers. 'He was anxious
to spend his money on something that would last for years and help
his education, too.'
'Yes, that's all very well, but—' his mum tried to interject.

'You must be so proud of him,' Mr Petrovsky said, smiling even more.

'Oh yes, we are, but—'

'I can see just how well brought up he is. And so polite, too. I must congratulate you.'

'Oh well—well, thank you,' replied his mum, lost for words and grinning back at Mr Petrovsky like a large Cheshire cat.

Tommy took his parcel, catching Mr Petrovsky's wink as he did so, and clutched it tightly to him. He had won this battle with the help of his newly-found friend.

At that moment, Sally staggered around the corner with her arms full of toys and plonked them on the shop counter.

'Mummy, I can't decide what I want, so it's probably best if I take them all.'

'Well, darling, it is rather a lot of toys.'

There was silence for a few seconds as Sally assessed the situation through angry, squinted eyes. Her chubby face was starting to turn a shocking shade of cerise.

'But I want all of them,' she said, her voice growing louder.

'Can't you just choose a couple, Sally, sweetheart?'

'A couple! How can I choose a couple when I want them all? All of them. You said I could have what I wanted, and this is what I want. And I want one of those, too.' She stamped her foot hard on the floor and pointed to a large bin at the front of the store.

'I want one of those T-shirts. A pink one!' she shouted and tearing over to the bin, started pulling the shirts out and tossing them onto the floor. 'This one. This one here. I want this and all the other toys, too.' She hurled herself to the ground, screaming and hitting the floor with her flailing fists.

Tommy's mum looked over at him. 'Do something, Tommy, please,' she said in a tight voice that sounded like someone had stuck a cork in her mouth.

Tommy glared at her. Why could his mum and Sally not just go away and leave him alone. 'Why can't *you* do something for a change?'

he sputtered, bile welling in his throat. Boy, he would be in trouble for that!

Sally's screaming had now surpassed supersonic level, and she started thrashing about on the floor.

'I'm not asking, I'm instructing,' spat his mum. 'She's going to have a fit if you don't stop her.' There was venom in his mum's voice—Tommy could hear it—but he could also feel her fear.

He looked at Sally, and again towards his mum, as fresh anger flooded into his veins. He could taste its acidity; feel its resentful grip. He wanted them to feel hurt like they hurt him. Only—

Yes, Sally was getting what she wanted—the way she knew how—and he would sort it out. Again. He hated the fact she was younger than him and as spoilt as a new-born baby. But she was still his sister. Most of all, he hated the fact that sometimes her screaming fits would turn into real fits. Epilepsy, his parents told him as they had shown him what to do in a real emergency.

He could see his mum's eyes squinting at him. Pleading with him? But his feet were glued to the floor. He wanted to help, but he was helpless himself, unable to take even one step forward.

Out of the panic and fear came a soft, low indistinguishable voice. The words it spoke were unfamiliar to Tommy. Mr Petrovsky walked calmly to Sally's side and knelt beside her. He closed his eyes and took a long, deep breath. Then, placing his hands wide open, he traced slow circles in the air above her, moving slowly upwards towards her head. He seemed to be chanting a spell.

'*Rebenok tishiny, bud'te spokojny. Tihij teper.*'

Sally gave a final lurch and then slumped on the floor—silent— her writhing body tranquil at last. Mr Petrovsky touched her forehead, murmuring once more.

'Hush, quiet one. Find the path again, and peace will follow.' He turned towards Tommy's mum and, placing his finger to his mouth for quiet, rose and went to her side.

'Take her home, Mrs Turner. She's tired. I'll wrap these things quickly if you like, but what Sally really wants is some calm and quiet.'

'Oh yes. Yes,' Tommy's mum replied, 'do that, please. I've—' she hesitated. 'I've never seen anything like that. How did you calm her?'

'Don't worry, Mrs Turner. Just something my grandmother taught me many years ago.' He turned to Tommy. 'Come and help me pack these things, while your mother sorts out Sally.'

Tommy was still staring at Mr Petrovsky. He could not believe what he had witnessed. Nobody had ever been able to pacify Sally in only a few seconds. But Mr Petrovsky had. This old, wizened, white-haired man was the most amazing person he had met in his life.

'Come, come, Tommy,' said Mr Petrovsky, softly. 'Let your mother do her duty. Come and help me.' He leant forward, his voice lowering to almost a whisper. 'Sally's not the only special one, you know.'

Tommy shrugged his shoulders. He had forgotten what special felt like.

'Don't ever underestimate what you can do, Tommy,' continued Mr Petrovsky. 'Open your mind, and you can be, can do, anything. Anything. You just have to believe.'

'But I don't know how to believe, anymore,' said Tommy quietly.

'Ah well, that's just it, you see. There's nothing to know. You just have to believe in yourself totally and absolutely. Everyone in the world is capable of extraordinary things. Of even changing the course of history. They just have to believe it is possible.'

The words Mr Petrovsky spoke wove their magic into Tommy. They enveloped him in a bubble of hope and possibilities. *Anything is possible.* That is what Mr Petrovsky had said. *You just have to believe.*

His eyes met the old man's kind gaze, and he saw in him the truth and sincerity of his words. No one had ever spoken so truly to him before or allowed him to dare to believe he could be special.

The question tumbled out of his mouth before he could stop. 'Who are you?'

Mr Petrovsky smiled mischievously. 'Do you really want to know?'

Tommy nodded in excitement.

'Well, come back and see me soon.'

Tommy grinned back at him. 'Do you mean that, really? Can I come back and see you?'

'Of course, you can, anytime.' Mr Petrovsky lowered his voice slightly. 'Oh, and Tommy, if you find an extra something in your package, use it well.'

✑ Chapter 5 ✑

A Trip to Yorintown

It was now seven-thirty, and supper was over in the Turner household. Tommy had just finished drying the dishes and was putting the last bowl away in the top cupboard. He hoped he could soon sneak away to his bedroom: his mind was going into overdrive. What could the 'extra something' be that Mr Petrovsky told him about? How could he 'use it well'?

Tommy's mum, meanwhile, was upstairs tending to Sally by feeding her an enormous bowl of chicken soup. Sally had gone straight to bed the moment they arrived home, and Tommy had seen his mum only once since then, when he had taken the food upstairs. Supper had been a very meagre affair of cheese and stale bread with just him and his dad, who insisted on teaching Tommy all about market shares while they were eating. His dad had done considerably well with some share dealing that day and had opened a dusty bottle of wine to celebrate, which, as usual, he was consuming rather too rapidly.

With the last counter wiped clean, Tommy headed for the kitchen door.

'I'm going upstairs to finish my homework, if that's okay with you?'

His dad shrugged nonchalantly as he made his way to the lounge, wine glass in hand. Tommy took that as a 'yes' and hurried off.

Out in the hallway lay the pile of packages from Petrovsky's Toy Store. Tommy picked up the largest parcel, which he knew contained the Space Station Kit, and rushed upstairs to his room. Once inside, he yanked off the paper bag and tossed the kit onto his bed. A piece of grey cloth tumbled onto his already cluttered bedroom floor. Tommy picked it up and saw it was a T-shirt. Was this the extra something Mr Petrovsky had placed in the package? A T-shirt? It seemed unlikely. Tommy peered into the bag, but nothing more was lurking inside. And Mr Petrovsky had said he must 'use it well.' What did he mean by that? It seemed a bit of a silly thing to say about a T-shirt. A flutter of disappointment went *flap* inside him. Perhaps it was a joke Mr Petrovsky liked playing on gullible kids, like him.

But still, he had his new Space Station Kit. Now that *was* exciting.

Tommy jumped onto his bed, opened the box and shook out the contents: rocket, launch pad and space station assembly kits, a book about planets, three astronauts and a variety of strange alien creatures tumbled onto his duvet cover. Tommy sorted through the pile then decided to start with the book. He knew the main facts about all the major planets by heart but was eager to learn more. He placed the other items back in the box, leant back on his pillow and started to read about Mars, the red planet.

Ten minutes later, there was a tap on the door and his mum poked her head round.

'Lights out time, Tommy. Teeth brushed? No. Undressed? No. I'll give you two minutes and no dawdling around. Oh, and wear something warm, it's getting cold these nights.'

'Okay, Mum,' he replied, getting off the bed in order to undress.

Tommy looked at the T-shirt lying abandoned on the floor. Mr Petrovsky's words skittered through his head, 'a special something', 'use it well.' Why would he say that? He had not seemed the sort of person to play a nasty trick. Tommy picked up the shirt and laid it carefully on his bed. *Perhaps there* is *something special about the T-shirt, only I cannot see it?* he thought, heading to the bathroom. *Perhaps Mr Petrovsky is telling the truth?* he thought, through a mouthful of toothpaste. *There's only one way to find out,* he concluded as he jumped into bed, flicked off the light and pulled the T-shirt over his head.

*

'Landing confirmed for 16:00 hours, over.' The voice crackled over the loudspeaker.

Silence.

'Do you copy? Over.'

Tommy woke with a start, disorientated by the voice. His room was pitch-black and weird whirring noises were coming from the end of his bed.

'Dad?' he whispered. 'Is that you?'

'Turner. Do you copy? Over,' said the voice, louder now and with a hint of frustration.

Tommy fumbled for the light switch, which was not in its usual place, found it and clicked it on. The sudden light dazzled him, dancing before his eyes in a multitude of colours. Blinking back watery tears, he tried to shake the fuzziness out of his head. But the colours kept on dancing. Eventually, his sleepy eyes focused and, letting out an enormous gasp, he stared in shock at what they saw.

Ahead of him, with hundreds of flashing lights and buttons, was a huge metallic cockpit stretching far out to either side of him. Above the instrument panel, a large dial rotated at high speed, its numbers rapidly descending. Tommy was sitting in a red leather swivel chair that felt as though it had been moulded around his body; a tightly buckled belt kept him well secured. The whirring noise came from a giant screen above the cockpit that was expanding inch by inch, revealing a picture of many millions of glimmering stars. On the right side of the screen a huge red ball was appearing, orange mists swirling and whirling, twisting and turning around it. It was getting nearer and nearer every second.

Tommy could not believe how vivid his dream felt. Every sound buzzed like electricity. Every colour sparkled as brightly as a jewel. But how on earth was he going to fly a spaceship with no one else to help him? Even if it was a dream.

Before he could take a calming breath, a black button on the left arm of his chair started to blink.

'Turner, are you there? Do you copy? Over.'

Tommy looked around in panic. Everything was happening far too quickly. The black button stopped flashing, so without thinking, he pressed it and spoke into a large microphone mounted in front of him.

'Ah, yes—Turner here.' His voice trembled with terror and excitement. 'Umm—what's going on? Umm—Over!'

'Going on? What do you mean, going on! You're landing in ten minutes. Where's the rest of the crew? Where's Peters?'

'I'm not—'

At that moment, a door banged behind him. Spinning around, he saw an enormous man come striding into the room. The man was dressed from head to toe in a silver suit and was carrying a child's beaker full of tea.

'What's going on, Turner?' he asked sleepily. 'What's the face for?'

Tommy, realising his mouth was hanging wide open in a silent scream, stammered, 'I think we're—umm—meant to be landing in—umm—ten minutes. Apparently.'

'Ten minutes,' yelled the immense man. 'Why didn't you wake me?'

Tommy could think quite clearly why he had not woken him. It was because he was asleep himself at this very minute, halfway through an utterly strange but entirely realistic dream. But he did not think he should say this right now.

'Never mind, reprisals later,' continued the man. 'Why isn't Ground Control in contact yet?'

The black button started blinking again, and the voice bellowed, 'This is Ground Control! What's going on there, Peters? Over.'

'Yeah, Peters here,' said the enormous man, grabbing control of the microphone. 'No probs, everything's cool.'

Without warning, the spaceship reeled to the right, hurtling downwards like a massive chunk of rock. Peters, shooting round to the other side of Tommy, jumped into another red chair, grabbed a big metal stick in front of him and swung it to the left.

'Brake, Turner!' he shouted. 'We're coming in too fast.'

Tommy scanned the array of knobs, unable to distinguish one from the other, his fingers running from one button to the next. On the screen the big red ball looked gigantic, looming ever closer. The ship lurched again, then plunged into the cloud of orange smoke he had seen wafting around the ball.

'We've hit the atmosphere,' yelled Peters. 'Where's the brake? The green lever. Pull it. NOW!' Peters smashed his hand onto a massive blue button as Tommy wrenched the green lever with all his might and a loud siren rang out around the room.

The ship reeled to one side, then righted itself, slowing swiftly to a normal speed. The dial he had spotted earlier showed the figure 4.57.43.

'Less than five minutes to go,' said Peters. 'Where's the rest of the crew?'

'Here, Skipper,' replied a voice behind him, and five more people came rushing into the room.

'Sorry we're late,' said another, strapping himself into one of the seats at the back of the room. 'We were feeding the Anjulongs, and you know how long that takes.'

'Four minutes and counting,' said Peters.

Tommy felt a sudden surge of adrenaline rushing through his body. *Where am I going*, he wondered, *and more to the point, what or who are the Anjulongs that took so long to feed?*

Peters had now taken control of the landing, and his only instruction to Tommy was to keep an eye on the braking system, which thankfully, Tommy now knew where to find. The orange haze, which had temporarily concealed the landing pad, was waning into wispy strands. Up ahead, Tommy could vaguely make out some lights flashing repetitively, like a line of lighthouses leading the way to safety.

'Two minutes and counting,' said Peters.

Everything's under control, thought Tommy, relaxing into his chair. *It's quite fun, this spaceship stuff. Easy-peasy when you know what button to press.*

Just then, a huge silver object flashed past the window. It looked like an enormous undulating balloon, changing shape before his very eyes. Round, then oval, concave, then round again. It doubled back on itself and charged towards the ship. Then came another from the opposite side. And another, this one gold in colour.

The first balloon struck the right side. *BAM!* Ship shuddering, lights flickering. Tommy's heart thumping, head pounding. Then on the left. Now on the roof. What was attacking them so near their destination?

'Landing disks attached,' stated Peters. 'Hit the brakes, Turner. Thirty seconds and counting.'

Tommy, letting out a sigh of relief, yanked the green lever again, and the ship ground to a halt, floating high up in the sky and suspended by the three landing disks. Slowly, steadily the ship descended, finally reaching the ground and safety.

'Good landing, folks,' said Peters. 'Now, we have ninety minutes decompression time before entering Yorintown, so I suggest you all retire to your bunks and get some shuteye.'

He turned to Tommy, smiling. 'Congrats, Turner. First mission completed. Now all we needa do is deliver the Anjulongs, and we're outta here.'

Tommy Turner's Tremendous Travels

৯ Chapter 6 ৶

The Anjulongs

The rest of the men unstrapped themselves and headed for the door. Tommy jumped down from his seat and followed them through and into a corridor that circled the control room. The door snapped shut behind him, its metallic *thud* echoing down the narrow walkway. Up ahead, the men were descending through a hatch. Tommy hurried after them.

Down below, they made their way along an identical corridor that circled the outer rim of the ship. Periodically, Tommy came to a door that read 'Engine Room' or 'Kitchen' or some such thing. One door, which looked stronger and firmer than the others, read 'Visitors.' A whiffy aroma of bad eggs blended with unwashed sweatpants and school dinners seemed to be wafting around this part of the corridor. Tommy hesitated for a moment. Itching to open the door and find out what was inside but fearful he would lose the others, he hurried onwards.

They must have walked almost halfway around the ship's perimeter when two of the men said goodbye and disappeared through a door. Another two took the next door, and at the third, the last man turned to Tommy. 'Here we are, Turner. Home sweet home.'

Tommy glanced at the sign on the door, which read *Baxter, Turner.* Why was his name on the door? The hairs on the back of his neck tingled in trepidation. It gave him the creeps. How did they know it was he? How did they know he was there? And, come to that, where was *there* exactly?

'Are you coming then?' Baxter's voice sounded muffled from inside. Tommy took a deep breath and scanned the corridors right and left. Nothing. No one. No choice but to stick with Baxter, for the time being, at least.

The room was minuscule and almost completely bare except for a bunk bed and two chairs on one side. A shower cubicle, wash area and small locker area had been placed opposite. Baxter threw himself onto the bottom bunk, stretched loudly, then took off his shoes. Tommy sat on one of the chairs, hoping his roommate would not fall straight to sleep; there was too much he wanted to know.

Baxter looked round at him. 'Good job today, Turner. I think the skipper likes you. So, this is your first time to Yorintown?'

'Yes,' replied Tommy, 'and yours?'

'Oh no, I've been here a couple of times now. We seem to be getting a lot of Anjulongs visiting Earth these days, and this crowd are apparently VIPs. Came down to talk at the Universe Summit or something like that. Mind you, they're a rowdy lot. Were up half the night partying yesterday. Didn't you hear them?'

'No,' said Tommy, thinking quickly. 'I must have been sound asleep the whole night.'

'That you were,' said Baxter. 'Well, wait 'til we're decompressed, and then we can get these creatures back to their city. One good thing about Yorintown, they always make us welcome. Not like some of the planets I've been to.'

Tommy's mind was racing with all the information Baxter had given him. Aliens visiting Earth to speak at a summit? Was he part of some vast intergalactic taxi service then? But surely, they could not be real? This could not be real? But then why did it all feel so real? He pinched himself on the arm—ouch—yes, that really was real. *But then how did I get here? And more importantly, how will I get back?*

'Baxter—' he asked, his voice sounding smaller than usual, 'what year is it now?'

'Why, Turner, it's 3018, can't you remember?' Baxter laughed. 'Now let's get forty winks before it's too late, shall we?'

*

The siren rang loudly around the cabin. Baxter woke with a snort. Tommy sat up, swung his legs off the top bunk and jumped to the floor. He had not managed to get a wink of sleep, but instead he had used the time to come to a conclusion; he must have eaten far too much cheese at supper and was now trapped in some weird extended dream. Once he had decided this, he was far too eager to find out what would happen next to try and snooze. Besides, Baxter had fallen asleep the moment his head hit the pillow and had snored dreadfully the whole time.

With a stretch and a yawn, Tommy ambled over to the sink and peered into the mirror. What a shock he got, for staring back at him was a young man. Granted, he looked a bit like him—the same messy hair and blue eyes—but his freckles had disappeared and stubble was growing around his chin. Gently, he reached up and touched his face, feeling chiselled bone and sandpaper skin. His hand seemed much larger than he remembered.

He was about fifteen years older than he had been when he had gone to bed in his house in Parsons Court. He loed down at his older body, dressed in the same silver suit Peters wore, and for the first time since his adventure had started, he wondered if he was actually awake. That this was not the vivid dream he had earlier believed it to be but that, somehow, he had fallen into a parallel dimension. *What if I cannot get back?* Yes, it was fun to be discovering new things aboard a spaceship a thousand years into the future, but he was really rather homesick. *What will Mum and Dad think if I don't show up at breakfast tomorrow? Will they go and look for me?* A peculiar lump went twang in his chest when he thought about his mum. It made him feel a bit weird. It made him sort of miss her, and—dare he say it—Sally, too. Just a little, of course. Maybe it was even a little bit scary? Suddenly having to be an adult and all that.

On the other hand, thought Tommy, *at least I won't have to face the Higgins Twins on Monday.* He looked again at his new face and stroked the rough stubble on his chin until Baxter broke into his thoughts.

'Okay, Turner, we need to go get those Anjulongs.'

Tommy followed Baxter back down the outer corridor. Peters was up ahead hurrying along. He stopped in front of the *Visitors* door and, after a purposeful knock, waited to be admitted. The others had just caught up with him when the door slid open, and in they all stepped.

Tommy had tried to prepare himself for yet another surprise, but what he saw inside the room was astonishing.

The chamber was huge and lavishly furnished in a baroque style, with lots of red velvet curtains and large, gold-framed oil paintings. *This must be the visitors' sitting room*, he thought, craning his neck so he could peek through an open door into one of the equally rich bedrooms. Inside the room the smell he had noticed earlier was overwhelming. It ponged like a dozen pairs of smelly socks worn for a week without washing. It was as much as he could do not to retch as he breathed it in.

The Anjulongs were positioned in various parts of the room and seemed to be thoroughly enjoying the generous hospitality being shown to them. Two were busy playing cards at a side table. Another was sitting with his feet up, drinking a beer and watching TV, while the largest member of the group was reclining on a chaise lounge, smoking a cigar. He was dictating a letter to the final member of the party, who sat at his feet taking notes.

They were quite simply the strangest bunch of aliens Tommy had ever seen. Not that he had actually seen any in real life before. They were bright blue, and each had three long giraffe necks, on each of which sat a head. On the centre neck was a huge round head that sported a pair of large, round eyes, while on top of the right-hand neck was a smaller head and mouth. Their jumbo-sized ears almost concealed the tiny head on the last remaining neck. They also had no nose, which could explain why they did not seem to mind the smell

that arose from them. They were dressed in safari kit (which Baxter later explained to Tommy was their Earth-visiting ceremonial gear), and the reason feeding time had taken so long was explained by the size of their vast, extended stomachs, which stuck out over the top of their shorts like camel's humps.

They were without doubt very, *very* ugly.

As Tommy and the others entered the room, the Anjulong who had been taking notes leapt to his feet and headed towards them, his necks wobbling with each heavy step.

'That's the official translator,' whispered Baxter to Tommy. 'The others are the ambassador's personal guards.'

'The ambassador is anxious to disembark this vessel as soon as is feasible,' he said in flawless English, his voice sounding like a 1950s newsreader. 'He has another engagement to grace with his presence prior to the gala tonight.'

As he finished speaking, the large Anjulong rose from his chaise lounge and, after puffing a huge smoke ring from his cigar, announced, 'Iya talkey nouw. Iya speeky da Ingleesh gut, yah.'

'Ambassador!' gushed the translator with pride. 'What a joyous occasion to heed such flawless pronunciation.'

'Seelence!' ordered the ambassador. The Anjulong flinched at this rebuff and hung his heads dejectedly.

Peters stepped forward and held out his hand to the ambassador. 'Welcome back to Yorintown, sir. We are now ready to leave the craft and transportation is waiting outside. If you will all follow me, we can go without any further ado.'

The ambassador snapped his large, blue fingers, and the other Anjulongs leapt to their feet, rushing over to form a tight ring around him. What a sight it was, all their heads and stomachs sticking out in different directions. Another finger snap, and Peters set off, leading the way through the ship. The Anjulongs shuffled along behind him, steadfast in their formation, clomping and wobbling their way until they reached the lift. With a bit of jostling, everyone crammed in, and the doors slid smoothly together. The Anjulong stench in the visitors' quarters had been pretty unbearable, but in this confined space it was truly disgusting. It smelt like someone had shovelled a stack of revoltingly rancid, dreadfully decomposing elephant dung into the lift, mixed in a few dead rats for good measure and then let the concoction mature for six months like a vintage cheese. Now it was at its ripest point—and it seemed they were trapped inside the slowest, deepest lift in the entire solar system. Tommy felt that, if he had to hold his breath much longer, his lungs would explode and he would end his days as a sticky mess all over the lift.

But at last the lift clunked to the ground floor, the doors opened and out they all burst, Tommy and the other astronauts gulping in that much needed fresh air. Then onwards they marched to the exit and out into Yorintown.

Tommy Turner's Tremendous Travels

✎ Chapter 7 ✐

Ambassador Anjulong's Party

The heat of the sun hit Tommy as soon as he had descended from the craft. He gazed up into the orange sky and then back towards the spaceship, so he could examine it. It was shaped like a huge, metal mushroom. They were standing at the bottom of the stalk, the rest of the ship looming way above them. Written on the side of the stalk was the word 'Galactiride' and a web address starting with the letters U.W.W. *I bet it means Universe Wide Web or something like that*, thought Tommy. The landing disks, now deflated, hung limply from where they had attached themselves.

The ship had landed on a very tall metal peak from which Tommy could get an excellent view of the city of Yorintown. It spread out as far as the eye could see and way beyond. Each gigantic building was suspended in midair and linked together by a series of roads.

'Where's the ground?' Tommy whispered to Baxter.

'Oh, it's there alright. It just takes a while for the human eye to see it,' he replied.

Floating by the edge of the peak was their transportation. It looked surprisingly like an old London sightseeing bus.

'They took the idea from our Earth history books,' explained Baxter. 'This way they have much more space for their necks, you see.'

They squeezed and squashed themselves inside with rather too much pushing and shoving, especially from the burly guards, and quick as a flash were off. It was a truly peculiar sight to see. The Anjulongs' heads stuck out of the open roof, with the ambassador taking centre stage and trying his hardest to look important. The translator held up a bright blue helium balloon on which was printed an elaborate crest: three large fire-coloured crowns encircled by glimmering ornate swirls.

Tommy guessed correctly that this was their equivalent of a royal emblem.

As the bus rushed past the tall buildings, many of the Anjulong public waved and cheered as they went about their daily business. Tommy waved back until he caught a glare from Peters that told him it was not the done thing.

Pretty soon they arrived at a large, important looking building. *It must be the embassy*, thought Tommy, spying an even larger balloon floating from a flagstaff outside the entrance. As they disembarked, Tommy inspected the building, trying to soak in every last detail.

The embassy towered way above them: fifteen, twenty floors at least. It was fashioned entirely out of large amber chunks that made the walls shimmer like iridescent crystal goblets, shooting back rays of sunlight as though the building was engulfed in flames. Tommy stood there in awe, his eyes bulging at the magnificence before him. On the top floors, long leaded-glass doors opened onto golden, jewel-encrusted balconies. Each one was lovingly crafted and hewn from material he could not name, or even comprehend—alien rocks and minerals had never part of his geography lessons. They seemed to be pulsating, swelling and receding in unison as though the whole building was breathing, living, alive—they looked like gills on a colossal copper fish.

Surrounding the palace, beautifully manicured gardens sprang forth. Flower heads the size of dinner plates bobbed in the breeze, and the summer sound of hungry insects filled the air. Majestic ostrich-like creatures wandered freely to and fro, pecking at the lawns—caw-cawing softly to each other.

In the centre of the driveway stood an immense statue that appeared to be of the ambassador himself, dressed in what looked like a Roman toga. His three heads were held aloof in a superior statesmanlike pose as though he was peering down his nose at the crowd before him. *If he actually had a nose to peer down,* thought Tommy, with a chuckle. In one hand, the ambassador was holding a clear, round bauble that spun continuously, twinkling in the sunlight. Within the bauble were other small globes of varying sizes, also spinning around themselves and each other. And when Tommy looked closely, he could see each was highly detailed, with seas and mountains and their own atmospheres. And there—Tommy stared again—there it was. A tiny orb named Earth. His home. He imagined his parents tucked up in bed, asleep. *Do they ever dream of flying spaceships?* he wondered. Next to the planet was a description that read:

Discovered in 2635 by
Thunskare Zapermoumous.
Inhabited by strange, single-necked race called Humans.
Joined the Universe Union in 2750.

Tommy glanced up and, seeing the rest of the party marching towards the embassy, hurried onwards. He was just catching up with them when two hefty guards threw open the colossal front doors and in they went, the immense foyer swallowing them whole like Jonah inside his whale. The gala was already underway. The party noise deafening. It looked as though all the best Anjulong society folk were attending. There were tiaras and coronets. There were glittering ball gowns and sparkling robes. There were bands playing and wild dancing every which way he looked.

'Youse injoyee da partee,' said the ambassador and was whisked away, with his bodyguards close by.

'Come on, everyone, let's mingle,' said Peters, and he, Baxter and Tommy squeezed their way through the raucous throng to the main ballroom.

Inside the ballroom, things were hotting up even more. The dance floor was packed with couples jiving, their lithe necks twisting this way and that as they kept the beat of the intricate dance. The music was infectious, filling Tommy with happiness and laughter and sweeping the three astronauts, feet tapping, to the edge of the dance floor. A waiter squeezed his way towards them with a large tray full of amber goblets. They each took a cup and toasted to their successful voyage. The liquid tasted sweet and burned Tommy's throat as he gulped it down, making him cough and splutter like an old tractor engine.

'Whoa now, Turner,' said Baxter. 'Powerful stuff this, 'ul knock you out cold if you're not careful.'

'What is it?'

'Blood of the Wungalat fruit. Bit like our rum, but more powerful.'

Tommy, who was already feeling tired and rather light-headed, decided one goblet of this delicious, intoxicating nectar was more than enough.

A middle-aged, portly man—the only Yorintown human Tommy had seen—appeared at their side, laughing with joy as he held his arms out to Peter.

'Good to see you, old chap. Must be ages since you were last over.'

He shook Baxter's hand warmly, welcoming him, too, then turned to Tommy.

'And who is this young fellow?'

'Turner. He's the newest member of our crew. Just graduated from Cambridge. Best in his class,' replied Peters.

'Good to have you on board, Turner. I'm Peeves-Withers, the Earth ambassador for Yorintown. Must say, its jolly good to see some old faces again,' he added, turning to the others.

Tommy glanced at the guests whizzing by. Before he knew it, a large blue hand had appeared out of the hurtling throng and Tommy was yanked into the rabble, his Anjulong dance partner twirling him this way and that to the music's beat.

The Anjulong fluttered her eyelashes at him and pouted her large glossy lips.

'Welcome to Yorintown,' she purred, giving him an enthusiastic whirl that made him feel hot and faint. He knew he had to get out of the crowd fast; first the Wungalat blood and now all this spinning was making him feel queasy, like he had just scoffed a kilo of pick 'n' mix. In a flash, the music changed to a loud jungle beat, and the crowd roared with excitement, swinging their heads in rhythm with the bongo drums. Without warning, Tommy's partner picked him straight off the ground and threw him into the centre of the crowd. He was caught by another Anjulong, who spun him around and then threw him again, high into the air.

One second, Tommy was upside down, looking at the crowd below, then he was rushing towards their outstretched arms, up again, narrowly missing the enormous chandeliers and hurtling back downwards, his stomach churning with the speed of it all. On and on this went, the whole dance floor stamping their feet and clapping their hands in time with the music until Tommy had no clue where or what or who he was. As he was hurtled towards the edge of the crowd, he could see Peters and Baxter standing at the side of the dance floor, laughing and joining in the revelry. Baxter was shouting something to him, but all Tommy heard was '—on't worry—me, too—traditional welcome—' then he was whisked out of range.

At last, the music changed back to a more subdued tempo, and Tommy was placed gently back on the ground, the Anjulongs around him calling out their greetings. The room spun uncontrollably. The floor dipped up and down like a fairground ride. Another minute and he would collapse with exhaustion. Excusing himself, Tommy pushed through the crowd until he had reached the edge of the room and plonked himself down on an empty chair. The room was still spinning, and so was his stomach. Peters and Baxter were somewhere over on the far side of the room, but standing up was not an option, let alone trying to find them. He felt giddy and alone amid the heaving crowd.

'Time to get you upstairs,' said a kindly voice. Tommy looked up at Peeves-Withers. 'It's usual on your first visit to get rather overwhelmed. The Anjulongs certainly know how to party, don't you think?'

Tommy smiled half-heartedly in agreement.

Peeves-Withers led the way from the room, up one grand set of stairs after another. They passed along thickly carpeted landings, where the walls told stories of past Anjulongs at battle and, more recently, of peaceful times. Portraits of fierce looking warriors, their eyes glinting meanly at Tommy as he tiptoed by. Pictures of finely dressed ladies, smiling and laughing as if they were saying, 'Stop a while and talk'.

At each turning, the party noise grew quieter until at last, as they entered through a heavy oak door, it was no more than a distant memory. Inside was nothing but a rich, peaceful silence.

'They keep this wing especially for Earth people, so you shouldn't find anything too unusual,' said Peeves-Withers. 'Now here we are. Just go in and make yourself at home.'

He reached into his top pocket, took out a small flask and gave it to Tommy. 'A souvenir from Yorintown,' he said. 'A couple of sips will have you right as rain in no time.' Then he bid Tommy farewell and strode off back to the party.

Tommy found himself in a magnificent room with an enormous, welcoming bed. At the far end of the room three tall windows looked out over the city of Yorintown. Opening the middle one, he stepped onto the amber balcony.

The gentle breeze felt cool on his hot, pink cheeks. Way below, the party noise was spilling out into the gardens, and several guests wandered through the grounds, taking in the night air. He looked at the glittering lights of the city, this strange city from another time, another world. The world of his dreams.

Is it possible to sleep when I'm already asleep and dreaming? he mused, walking over to the bed and launching himself onto it. The soft blankets felt so inviting. *Maybe if I have a few minutes' snooze, I can return to the party and find out what happens next.* He took a sip from the flask, the liquid tasting like sweet strawberry marshmallows. Everything felt warm and cosy and very snuggly, as if he were floating in a velvety cloud. *It's far—toooooo—exciting to go home just yet,* he yawned, taking off his silver space suit and clambering beneath the sheets. He took another sip from the flask and laid his head on the silky pillows, his breathing slowing gently as he fell into a deep sleep.

Tommy Turner's Tremendous Travels

❧ Chapter 8 ❧

Questions and Answers

'Tommy. Tommy? Are you up yet?'

His mum's voice was ringing in his ears.

'You've five minutes to get down here before I clear the breakfast things away,' she called up the stairs.

Slowly, he opened one eye and then quickly closed it again. His head was pounding like crazy, and his whole body felt as stiff as a rod, as though he had been wrapped up overnight and mummified. He forced his eye open again and saw Sally standing over him, staring.

'Get up, lazy, unless you want big trouble.'

He tried opening his mouth to reply, but it felt like all his muscles had dissolved during the night, leaving him as lifeless as a rag doll. All he could manage was 'Gu'way' before slumping back onto his pillow.

'Well, if you want to spend all Saturday lazing around, that's fine. I've got better things to do.' Sally snorted and turned on her heel. Tommy heard her shouting downstairs to their mum that he was still in bed and his mum yelling up to him again, giving him one last chance.

Tommy lay motionless for a moment longer, summoning the strength to stand up. Every muscle ached and stabbed as if he had just done twenty rounds in a boxing ring. His crumpled bedclothes were soggy, and the grey T-shirt, which he must have pulled off during the night, was lying in a heap by his pillow.

But finally, he felt able to face his mum and breakfast. As he moved to the side of the bed in order to get out, his right leg brushed against a small object. Grasping hold of it, he saw it was a flask. The same flask he had been given at Ambassador Anjulong's party.

But of course, it can't be. It was just a tremendous dream I had last night, he thought, his head spinning like an overheated tumble dryer. *Wasn't it? Yes, of course it was just a strange dream. But why can I remember every single detail? The colours, the sounds, even that awful pungent Anjulong smell. And why do I feel so bad, if it isn't because of the Wungalat blood?*

The flask glinted in his palm. Solid, real, a fact. And one thing he knew for certain was that things do not become real from a dream.

What had happened last night?

I must find out the truth. But how? Who can I tell? He thought back to the strange events of the previous night. *Who can I show the flask to?* All of a sudden, it came to him. Mr Petrovsky, of course. Mr Petrovsky would know what to do. After all, he had helped Sally, and it must have been him who had given Tommy the T-shirt. *I'll go and see Mr Petrovsky straight after breakfast,* he resolved, hurrying to get ready.

*

CLANG went the doorbell as Tommy entered the shop. He had sped here on his bike as soon as he could, promising his mum he would be back by eleven-thirty, as they were visiting her brother, Uncle Harry that afternoon.

Mr Petrovsky was nowhere in sight, but Tommy, spying a spotty older boy by the cash desk, went over and asked if he was in.

The boy nodded and pointed to the stockroom stairs. 'Down there in the office.'

'Do you think I could see him?' asked Tommy, already heading towards the doorway.

'Don't see why not,' said the boy in a don't-really-care sort of way and went back to reading a computer magazine.

Tommy reached the bottom of the stairs just as Mr Petrovsky stepped out of his office.

'Ah, there you are,' he exclaimed. 'I've been expecting you. Come this way, in you go. Let me get you something to drink.' He led Tommy into the office, sat him down and poured him a large glass of orange squash. 'So, tell me, tell me. Why are you here? Did it happen already?' he asked anxiously, pulling a large rocking chair nearer to Tommy's and plonking himself down.

'I think so,' replied Tommy, surprised. 'Well, at least, I'm not sure what you mean, but the strangest thing happened to me last night.'

'Well then, best you tell me all about it, and then we can decide what to do.'

Tommy told Mr Petrovsky all about his adventure to Yorintown and the Anjulongs, starting with finding the T-shirt.

'You put it in my parcel, didn't you? You said I might find something.'

'Of course, it was me, who else!'

Mr Petrovsky's eyes grew wider and wider the more Tommy recalled. He kept muttering things like 'Better than I could have imagined' and 'I knew it the moment I saw you.'

When Tommy pulled out the flask, Mr Petrovsky threw his arms up in amazement and examined it with awe. 'I have never seen anything so beautiful in my whole life. Do you know what this means, Tommy? Do you truly understand? You are holding a treasure from our future. The future of humanity.'

'Mr Petrovsky—' Tommy hesitated, unsure what to say, 'why is this happening to me? I'm not really sure what it all means. Can you tell me what it means?'

Instead of replying straight away, Mr Petrovsky sat rocking back and forth, tapping his fingers together, deep in thought. Tommy wiggled on his chair, trying his best to be patient but much too excited to keep still. Eventually, the old man looked up.

'There are three important lessons to learn in life, Tommy,' he started. 'The first is courage—courage to accept a situation without knowing what the future will bring. Courage is the ability to face the unknown without giving way to fear.

'The second lesson is strength. Strength of body and mind to believe you will win, even when you fear the worst. To be able to withstand fright and know you will triumph in the end.'

'And the third? What can the third be?'

'Valour. The power to help and protect those around you.' Mr Petrovsky leant closer. 'Last night, Tommy, you learned the first lesson. You showed courage, even when you were frightened and unsure. Many people wouldn't have been as courageous as you were last night. They would have panicked and shown their fear, and then goodness knows what might have happened. But you, you kept your head straight, even though the strangest things were happening all around you.'

'But I thought I was dreaming, even though it felt so real.'

'That doesn't matter. What does matter is you learnt how to be in control of your own destiny. Remember this lesson well; keep it in your heart and make certain to use it in the future.'

'I will, Mr Petrovsky, I promise. But about the T-shirt? Why did you give it to me?'

'I'm glad you asked,' said the old man, leaning back in his chair. 'You see, that is the strange thing. When I found it I wasn't sure, but I could feel there was something special about it straightaway. It came to me right out of the blue about two weeks ago. What surprised me was how ordinary it was. Just an ordinary, boring, grey T-shirt. Anyway, I put it to one side and forgot all about it until the day you came into the shop. But the moment I saw you, I knew you were the one I had to give it to.'

'But why me? I don't think there's anything special about me,' said Tommy, his grin belying his casual reply.

'Let's call it an old man's instinct for now, shall we?' replied Mr Petrovsky. 'And Tommy, never underestimate who you are or what you can do.'

Mr Petrovsky got stiffly to his feet, rubbing his tired knees as he did so, and walked towards the door.

'Stay there. I'll be back in a minute.'

Tommy stayed in his seat, looking around at the piles of dusty old ledgers stacked against the wall. Inside his heart glimmered. *Maybe it is true*, he thought. *Maybe I, Tommy Turner, really am special.*

'Here we go then.' Mr Petrovsky re-entered the room, carrying with him a package. He sat back down and held it out to Tommy. 'For your treasures. I'd keep it locked at all times, if I were you.'

Tommy ripped off the wrapping, eager to find out what he had been given. Inside lay a painted box, inlayed with exquisite semi-precious stones and small chunks of marble. Only the finest craftsmen could have achieved such intricate detail. It looked as old as time, and most of the gold had been rubbed off by its former owners' hands, but its sheer beauty still took Tommy's breath away.

He stared at it nervously. *How can I take such a precious gift*, he thought, mesmerised by its splendour.

'I know what you're thinking, Tommy, but believe me, I have waited many years to find the rightful owner for this box, and there is no one better qualified than you. Please take it, treasure it, and may some of its magic rub off into your life.'

'But I don't know how to thank you for such a gift,' said Tommy. 'You have already given me more than you know, so I think we should end this discussion right here and now. Oh, and don't forget this.' Mr Petrovsky handed him a small but elaborately cast key tied onto a piece of string. 'Wear it around your neck. Never take it off, just in case.'

He looked up at the clock ticking away on the mantelpiece.

'I think you'd better be off.'

'Oh, crumbs, eleven-fifteen,' said Tommy, jumping to his feet. 'Thank you, Mr Petrovsky, thank you for everything.'

'I think I'll be seeing you again before very long, Tommy. Now off you go and remember what I have said.'

Tommy bounded up the stairs two at a time, but at the top he stopped and turned around. 'Mr Petrovsky, you said you would tell me who you are.'

'All in good time, Tommy. All in good time. Off you go now.'

๑ Chapter 9 ๏

A Visit to Uncle Harry

The journey up to Uncle Harry's was as dreary as a damp, grey day. Tommy's dad had tuned into the test match at Lords, and the radio had been blaring out boring commentary the whole way. His mum spent most of the time drumming her long, manicured nails on the armrest; the rest of it she spent nagging her husband.

'Next right junction, Gordon—mind that lorry—slow down, you're driving like a maniac.'

Sally, however, was unusually quiet. She just sat there in her new pink 'MAGIC!' T-shirt, sucking her thumb and clutching one of her dolls. Not a murmur had passed her lips for the duration of the trip. Not that Tommy minded. It gave him time to think about his morning conversation. 'Three lessons to learn,' Mr Petrovsky had said. That meant last night must be the first of many adventures. What would happen to him next? Would he discover other new planets, travel again into the future? Would he be strong enough to encounter the unknown and learn to become a hero? And still the burning question remained. *Why me?*

Eventually, they arrived at the turning to the rambling, ivy-covered mansion that had been home first to Tommy's great-grandparents, then his mum's parents, and which now belonged to Uncle Harry. The overgrown driveway hid the house right up until the last bend. Then there it was. Meadowhill Grange, standing in all its dilapidated Tudor glory. The gravel drive scrunched as the car slowed to a halt.

Uncle Harry was standing at the top of the stone steps, his hand resting on one of the marble lions guarding the entrance. He was peering through an enormous magnifying glass at a large patch of mildew growing on the lion's back.

Tommy jumped out of the car, raced up the steps and straight into Uncle Harry's outstretched arms.

'Good to see you, old chap.' Uncle Harry clapped him on the back and, stepping away, shook his hand with gusto. 'Got to do something with George here.' He pointed at the slimy, green cat. 'This whole place is disintegrating before my very eyes.'

The rest of the party joined them on the top step and, after much helloing and kissing and handshaking, they turned to go inside.

Uncle Harry was a confirmed bachelor. He had been for most of his forty-three years, and it was no surprise judging by his appearance. He was about as different to his sister as Tommy was to his own. At first glance he looked somewhat intimidating, being very tall and angular. His elbows and knees jutted out considerably as though his bones had grown longer than they should have. A mass of prematurely grey hair hung over his face, stopping halfway down his back where he had attempted to tie it in a ponytail. He walked with a slight stoop and stared attentively but somewhat alarmingly at everyone with his heavily hooded eyes. He was dressed in a tatty old golfing sweater that had once belonged to Tommy's dad, patched corduroy trousers and a pair of muddy Wellingtons. Tommy's mum had given up trying to smarten him up, and her attempts at finding him a suitable wife were long since over. She considered her brother an embarrassing bother and was grateful they lived far enough away that she did not feel obliged to invite him to her dinner parties.

Tommy, on the other hand, thought Uncle Harry was one of the coolest people he had met in his entire life. He wanted to be exactly like his uncle when he grew up, for Uncle Harry was an adventurer.

From the deserts of Arabia to the jungles of Malaysia, Uncle Harry had travelled, bringing back trinkets and stories of other worlds. Tommy could remember every memento that had been placed into his growing hands. An amulet from the Andes, a talisman from Tasmania, a curio from Cuba. Each piece a unique treasure. A rarity. A gift from another time. But what Tommy loved most of all were the stories. Tales of jungle tribes, desert people, fights with lions, and endless journeys to lost civilisations.

Each story was related to Tommy in secret when the rest of the family were having their afternoon snooze. His parents had no wish to acknowledge Uncle Harry's 'strange ways' as they put it. His mum, if pressed, would say he was a travel correspondent for a world-famous organisation.

Lunch was already prepared and waiting for them in the faded Great Hall. After freshening up from the trip, the family took their places at the enormous oak dining table. It was a ridiculous sight to see. Being the self-elected head of the family, Tommy's dad conceitedly insisted that he always sit at the top of the table. His mum, haughtily proud of her long ancestry, and still furious that Uncle Harry had inherited the family house, always insisted on sitting at the other end of the table. Sally had to sit by her side, so she could cut up dainty morsels for her daughter and persuade her to eat them. This left ten places on either side of the table to be filled by the remaining two, who normally sat together in the middle.

It was not exactly a cosy arrangement and did not bode well for a relaxing family meal. Tommy's mum kept demanding he pass the potatoes and veg, so he spent most of the time rushing from one end to the other with handfuls of hot dishes. His dad bellowed on and on to Uncle Harry about what stocks he should be buying right now, while Harry nodded vigorously, trying to look interested. Tommy's mum kept interjecting, shrieking things like, 'Take heed, Harry, free advice from a financial genius.'

Finally, after what seemed like an eternity, the last morsel was scraped from their plates. Tommy's dad retired to the library for 'a puff and a read' and his mum took Sally upstairs to change for a prearranged riding lesson.

'Let's go through to my study,' pronounced Harry, as soon as it was calm. 'I have something rather special to show you. Picked it up in Greece a couple of weeks ago on my way back from Kárpathos, and Tommy—' he paused dramatically. 'Tommy, I really think this time I have found gold!'

'What is it? What have you found,' said Tommy eagerly as they sped down the corridor.

'I'm not that sure yet, but I only hope it's what I think because if not, I will soon have to sell this place. I simply can't afford to keep running it. Look, I even had to sell old Hubert last month.' Uncle Harry pointed to an empty spot where an ancient suit of armour had once stood.

Arriving at the study, Tommy plonked himself down on the tattered old sofa and looked up at Uncle Harry, who was rummaging around in his travelling trunk. Tommy loved this room in all its tumbledown grandeur. He loved the musty smell, the piles of mysterious packages and the casual comfort of the badly sprung seats, but most of all he loved the oldness of it, far removed from the peach satin couches and cream carpets of his own home. It was crammed from head to toe with souvenirs from across the globe. Old maps adorned the walls, each littered with markings and pins proclaiming the destinations to which his uncle had journeyed. He felt as if this room had its own life. Its own stories to tell.

'Ah, here it is,' said his uncle, pulling out from beneath the jumble of things a roll of cloth tightly tied with rope. He brought the package over to Tommy, pulled off the fastenings, and laid it on his knee. 'Do the honours and tell me what you think.'

Tommy carefully pulled back the cloth, frightened to rush in case he dropped the treasure concealed within. It felt heavy and solid in his hand. The object was long and curvy and slightly pointed at one end. The other end looked as though it had been ripped directly from the ground, like the roots of a tiny tree stump. Tommy ran his fingers along the length of its undulating curves, trying to contain his disappointment. It looked like nothing but a silly lump of stone.

'Well, what do you think it is, then?' enquired Uncle Harry, smiling despite Tommy's lukewarm response.

'I'm not sure. It's… great,' Tommy said unenthusiastically, wondering how on earth this grey piece of stone could have made his uncle so excited.

Uncle Harry sat down beside Tommy and pointed at the object. 'What does it look like to you?'

Tommy thought for a moment. 'I suppose it looks a bit like a snake.'

'Bingo,' said Uncle Harry. 'Look at this end, slightly larger and flatter, with dents here where the eyes were. It was a snake alright, but that was many thousands of years ago'.

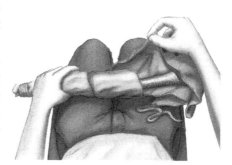

'A thousand years old—cool!'

'More like five thousand, and now it's fossilised.'

'A fossilised snake. But how can a fossilised snake bring you your fortune?'

Uncle Harry rubbed his hands together. 'Well, Tommy, I'm pretty sure only one other fossil like this one has ever found before. In 1873, a boy about your age discovered it while he was out climbing one day with some friends. If you ever go to Greece, you could see it in the National Museum in Athens. But no one has ever been able to identify what the snake was or how old it is. They did some tests on it about ten years ago, but—and this is the strange thing—it doesn't seem to have any DNA, which is impossible. Everything has DNA.'

'And you think you've found the second example, do you, Uncle Harry?' said Tommy, eagerly.

'Well, as I say, I'm pretty sure it's something special. Monday morning, I'm going to ring up my old friend Jolyon at the British Museum and pop down to London to show it to him. Maybe he can help me identify what it is.'

'I really hope he can help you, Uncle Harry.'

'So do I, so do I. Who knows, this could be the find of a lifetime.'

'But where did you find it?' Tommy asked, sitting forward in anticipation.

'That's the funny part, Tommy,' replied his uncle. 'I didn't find it. It found me.'

✎ Chapter 10 ✎

Uncle Harry's Adventure

'What do you mean, found you?' Tommy asked his uncle.

'Exactly that. Look, it's probably best if I start from the beginning and tell you everything. Then you can make up your own mind about what happened, although I must say I'm still as confused as you will be when you've heard my tale.'

Tommy snuggled into the tatty sofa and waited eagerly for his uncle to begin.

'As you know, I have been travelling through the Greek Islands for the last couple of months. I'll take you there one day, Tommy, and show you its beauty. There is so much ancient history and so many unspoilt landscapes, if you choose to get away from the tourists, that is.

'Anyway, I had chartered a small sailboat from the mainland. On most of the islands I managed to find shelter with a local farmer or fisherman, and I always paid for their hospitality by cleaning nets or picking figs or olives. Every morning, I would take time to bathe in the warm ocean waters. Sometimes I would dive so deep I could hardly breathe, and once I found an underground cave to explore. Now and again I would find a rusty tin mug or barnacled coin that hinted of ancient shipwrecks but nothing I would call priceless. So, you can imagine after four weeks I was getting rather frustrated.

'I decided to travel north towards Kithnos, where I wanted to take its healing waters. It was a warm, balmy morning, and the sun was hotting up as I rowed out to my sailboat with the fisherman who had been kind enough to let me lodge. I bid him farewell and took his offering of smoked fish, although to tell you the truth, I was rather tired of fish by this time. With a fair, warm breeze billowing up my sail, off I set in search of an adventure. Little did I know then what I would find.

'I had been sailing for about thirty minutes in a calm sea when I noticed the wind picking up. It could only have been a matter of minutes before a great dark cloud rose before me, rapidly enveloping the horizon beyond. At first, I was not alarmed; it was a long way off, and you know I have experienced strong seas a number of times. But before long, I started to feel quite uneasy; for this cloud was nothing like any I had ever seen before. It hung like a great albatross, hovering high above, waiting to catch its prey.

'The cloud lay about thirty minutes ahead of me, and so I decided to turn the boat round and head back. I reckoned I could stay ahead of the storm until I had reached safety. Without delay, I spun the boat around and set off in the opposite direction. But just as I was starting to relax, I noticed another cloud appearing on the horizon before me.

'I looked back at the first cloud, and my heart filled with fear; the cloud was closing in on me, trapping me between the two storms. All I could do was brave the tempest that was about to hit me. Quickly, I strapped a strong rope around my waist and another around the wheel to keep the boat on course. The waves were starting to swell with such ferocity I was sure any minute my boat would turn upside down and sink into the murky depths below.

'And then came the rain, lashing down in such torrents that within seconds I was drenched through. Boy, it was cold—so cold—but there was no time to shelter; I had to start bailing out water. The next twenty minutes are a blur, even now. All I remember is being enveloped in a thick fog, praying it would soon be over. I must have bailed out a hundred buckets of water. My arms ached all over. I could hardly stay upright on the slippery deck as the wind and waves howled around me, beating the life out of the little boat.

'I was too exhausted to care what would happen, and when I saw a large, black rock looming up ahead, I knew I was finished. The boat would be shattered against the rocks, and I would be tossed into the raging sea, my body smashed against the cliff face. Falling to my knees, I prayed with all my might for a miracle as I waited for the boat to hit the rocks. But it didn't. Instead, I found myself sailing through a narrow gap and into a large cave. Somehow—

unbelievably—I had missed the rock face. Outside, the storm was still raging, but within the shelter of the cave I was safe at last.

'A gentle tide pulled my little boat towards the back of the cave where the rocks narrowed and the ocean gave way to an underground river. On and on I drifted—for how long I don't know—for by then I had fallen into a deep, exhausted sleep.

'When I finally awoke, the boat had come to rest. All was pitch-black except the glow of phosphorus clinging to the rocks around me. The only sound was a gentle lapping of water against the shore. It was so peaceful after the tyrant storm that I felt I could stay forever in this womblike cavern. But I also knew I had to find my way back to civilisation. I groped my way into the cabin, lit an oil lamp for company, and swallowed down some pieces of dried fish. Oh, how wonderful that fish tasted. I shall never again complain of eating too much fish.

'I finished my meal and went back on deck to survey the storm damage, although I knew in my heart what the answer would be—considerable. The boat was beyond repair. It was a true miracle I had survived the storm but now I had to somehow get out of the cave and find a way off the island. I thought perhaps the fisherman I'd been staying with had seen the storm and sent a rescue boat to pick me up. But I had to get to a place where I could send a rescue flare. Quickly, I bundled together a few essentials and made my way to land.

'The rocks were steep to climb and slippery, too, from the seaweed and algae that clung to the sides. At first, I felt light-hearted—it was exciting to be heading on a new adventure—but after a while, the first thoughts of fear crept inside me. What if there was nobody to rescue me? The air was as still as death, and not a whisper of a breeze touched my skin. I felt lightheaded and dizzy, and my very bones ached with tiredness. I felt I would never find a way out of that rancid cave.

'I had decided to stop for a rest when I noticed a chink of light streaming through a crack in the rocks ahead of me. I can't tell you how much my heart leapt. In my joy, I bounded forward, forgetful of my weariness, only wanting to reach the light.

'That was where I made my mistake. I was almost there when I slipped on some loose stones and plunged into a deep chasm in the rocks. Down and down I fell, tumbling over and over, crashing against rock after rock. As I fell, I saw my life rushing past me, wave after wave of incidents spilling out into the unknown, and you, Tommy, I kept seeing you fading away into the distance. I thought I would never see you again, watch you grow into a man, share my secrets with you. I thought I would die.'

The room was silent as Uncle Harry stared mesmerised into the air, his body twitching as he relived every rock scrape and body bounce of his fall.

A ripple of fear shuddered up Tommy's back. Uncle Harry dead. No, that was unthinkable.

'What happened next, Uncle Harry?' he gulped, his voice sounding small after the enormity of his uncle's tale. 'How did you get out of the cave?'

Uncle Harry looked at Tommy. 'To this day I have not the faintest idea how I survived the fall or how I ended up in the Evangelismos hospital in Athens—'

'You ended up in hospital?' gasped Tommy, his stomach twisting into a knot.

'Yes, I did, but no matter now. Let me continue with my story, and perhaps you will understand what happened next.' Uncle Harry cleared his throat and began again.

'As I told you, the next thing I remember was waking up in hospital, surrounded by doctors and covered with tubes and pipes and all manner of paraphernalia. Now—and this is the strange part—there was not a scratch on my body!'

'Huh? How could that be after your fall? It's impossible.'

'I will never know, but all that was wrong with me was a state of utter exhaustion. I'd been fast asleep for the past week. The doctors were very kind. They had found me at the hospital entrance, all wrapped up in a cotton sheet like a mummy, and they had taken me in and managed to revive me. They couldn't identify me, because somewhere along the way, I'd managed to lose all my papers. Otherwise they'd have rung your mother, no doubt, and told her what was happening, and then no end of problems would have occurred, if you know what I mean.'

'That would have been the worst thing ever!' exclaimed Tommy, imagining the hysteria his mother would have worked herself into.

'But do you know, Tommy, that was not the strangest thing.'

'Why, what happened?' Tommy wiggled closer to the sofa's edge.

'Well, during the coma, I had an extraordinary dream. It was so real I felt I was living it. I dreamt I was lying at the bottom of the rocks, unable to move, bleeding heavily, and passing in and out of consciousness. I remember hearing a scraping noise as if a huge rock were being slowly rolled away. Then I heard whispering. At first, it was very distant, but gradually the whispering got closer until it was right by my head. I couldn't see anything, and I was too weak to cry out, so I stayed silent. But inside I was trembling with fear. I dreamt I was tenderly lifted and carried a great distance by three or four men. All the time the whispering continued, although what they were saying was beyond me. Their language was totally unknown to me.

'I dreamt I saw a crowd of people, their pale, waxy faces staring at me in wonderment, touching me with long, bony fingers. They drew ever closer, gaining confidence in their examination, when an old wizened man suddenly appeared. The crowd parted, swiftly dispersing behind the surrounding rocks. The old man leant near and held a flask of liquid to my lips. I was too weak to drink but managed to swallow a few sips. It tasted bitter in my dry mouth. Then he carefully dressed my wounds with ointment he extracted from a large stone pot.

'I must have dreamt about the old man twenty times. Each time was the same. He would make me drink the bitter liquid. Then he would dress my wounds. He never spoke, never uttered a sound, but the way he looked at me was enough. The depth of his eyes spoke more than any words ever could. They spoke of kindness and compassion. Of an ancient wisdom now lost in the modern world. Down there, under the rocks, the people lived a life as their ancestors had lived long ago, a secret sect who had no need of cars and computers, but who wished to be left alone to continue what their forefathers had started many hundreds of years before.

'And this is all I remember from the time I fell until I woke up in hospital. Nothing more, nothing less.'

Uncle Harry fell silent. Tommy's mind was awhirl with information. The boat, the storm, the island. The people and the old man. Was it a dream, or could they really exist? He thought about his dream with the Anjulongs. *Was* that a dream, too? *Can dreams really feel so real?* Or had his uncle actually fallen into a gorge that held a secret of past civilisations? And what about his uncle's fall? Had he died, would he ever have been found, or would he have just disappeared into thin air? How come he had not a single cut on him when he woke up in the hospital, and who could have found him if the old man did not exist?

Uncle Harry cleared his throat and, reaching forward, took the cloth roll from Tommy's hands.

'I'll put it away in the safe for now, I think,' he said, getting to his feet. 'Let's hope Jolyon has some good news for me when I go and see him.'

'But, Uncle Harry, you still haven't told me how you found the fossil.'

'That's right, I haven't. Well, it's really the most boring part of the story, but let me fill you in. Once I had woken, the doctors kept me in hospital for a couple of days just to check I was okay. When it was time for my release, they gave me my belongings, which they had found beside me on the hospital steps: my old rucksack and climbing boots. The fossil was buried beneath the things in my rucksack. I can't tell you how excited I was when I found it, but who put it there is yet another mystery in my adventure. Not that I mind really. Not if it makes me my fortune.'

'Do you think it could have been the old man?' gasped Tommy. 'You know, if he really did exist?'

'Who knows, Tommy? I just hope it is what I think.'

Tommy hesitated, a question burning on his lips. 'Uncle Harry, there's one thing I'm not sure about.'

'What's that then, Tommy?'

'Well, it's just that—how are you going to make anyone believe you?'

'Ah! Yes, well!' His uncle spun round from the safe, then sighed and sank like a burst balloon onto the floor. 'Yes, well, you see, that's the thing. I don't really know. Why would anyone believe me? How can I make them believe me when I don't even know for sure myself what happened?

'I shall be ruined, I know it,' his uncle continued, 'and your mother will take over the house and tell me I'm useless, and I am useless. I should have worked harder at school and become a banker like your father and married Fiona Billingsworth when I had the chance, but I didn't. I wanted to become an adventurer and travel the world. Well, just look at me now, washed up, penniless, and worthless. The greatest no-hoper in history—' He trailed off with a wail of despair, lost in a haze of self-pity.

'You are not useless.' Tommy jumped to his feet, knocking over a pile of manuscripts in his haste. 'You are not useless!'

He spun around the room, arms wide open, his eyes travelling from object to object. 'Look, Uncle Harry, just look. I think you're the most amazing person in the whole world. We'll find a way to prove this is like the other snake in the museum. We have to find a way; it's our only chance.'

Uncle Harry picked himself off the floor and sat down with a plonk on the nearest armchair. 'You're right, Tommy,' he said determinedly, 'there's no use getting all emotional about this. We have to think logically. Get the thing x-rayed for a start, and then we've got the DNA testing and all sorts of possibilities. That's it. Think straight.

We will find a way, and believe me, the world won't know what's hit them.'

He strode over to his desk and picked up the phone. 'First things first, Tommy. I won't wait until Monday. I think a phone call to my friend Jolyon right now will do the trick.'

And a little bit of magic wouldn't go astray, thought Tommy as Uncle Harry dialled the number.

*

For the rest of the afternoon, Uncle Harry shut himself away in his study, making numerous telephone calls and scribbling down all sorts of undecipherable notes. Jolyon, it seemed, was highly interested in what Uncle Harry had found and had told him to get the first train down to London on Monday morning, so they could start on the tests. He had rung back some ten minutes later, saying that on no account should Uncle Harry tell anyone of his find, and that it had already stirred up a great hornet's nest of excitement within the department. He had then rung again within five minutes to say that the chief of the Ancient Bones Department would be there to personally greet Uncle Harry, and that he should take a cab and not the train. They would cover all expenses, naturally.

Tommy stayed in the room for a while, listening to the chaos going on and occasionally picking up pieces of paper Uncle Harry knocked off the desk as he hurried about. Then, quite exhausted by the whole afternoon, he slipped quietly from the room and along the great corridor to the coolness of the garden outside.

He hurried down the ramshackle stone steps, through the decaying rose garden, past the overgrown beech hedge—gravel crunching at his feet with every step—and along the high wall that ran the length of the lawn. At last, hidden from sight by the ancient fruit trees, he reached the rotting wooden gate. It squeaked as he opened it and stepped inside. The gate sprang back into place behind him.

The small walled garden (once the vegetable plot, now sadly choked by weeds) lay dappled in the late afternoon sunlight. In the middle of the far wall stood a rickety grey wooden bench, which Tommy headed towards and sat upon. This was absolutely his most favourite part of Meadowhill Grange, apart from Uncle Harry's study, of course. It was the place Tommy escaped to whenever possible, especially if Sally was at her most annoying.

But today he had come here for a different purpose. He had come here to think about the extraordinary events that had taken place in such an unusually short space of time.

A couple of late summer butterflies fluttered merrily around the broken piles of flowerpots, but Tommy was in too much of a whirl to notice anything as mundane as that.

Space travel, Mr Petrovsky, fossilised snakes, Uncle Harry, the Anjulongs all came rushing into his head like a plate of tangled spaghetti.

In the past twenty hours he had landed a space taxi, drunk the blood of the Wungalat fruit, met a bunch of the weirdest aliens, held an immensely rare fossil, cheered up Uncle Harry and maintained an illusion of normality in front of his parents. Not bad going for someone whose only after-school activity was detention!

But somehow, he needed to put his thoughts into order. Sort out what he had control of, and could therefore alter if necessary, and what was completely and ridiculously out of his power to do anything about.

The flight to Yorintown, taking home the Anjulongs, well, it must have been a dream. Maybe the tiny flask had been part of the Space Station Kit he had brought at Petrovsky's Toy Store, and he had not noticed it when he tipped the contents onto his bed. But that did not really sound or feel right. The memories were too clear for it to have been merely a dream. And if so, why had Mr Petrovsky said he had been expecting him, and why had he not just laughed at Tommy's story? And why on earth had he given Tommy the T-shirt? No, these were things he had no idea how to organise in his head. He would just have to trust Mr Petrovsky and wait to see what happened next. The thought of whatever 'next' was gave him a funny feeling right in the lowest part of his tummy. The strangest kind of feeling, as though he had swallowed one of the butterflies. A very tiny one, mind you, but one which was now flapping about inside him.

He pushed the feeling away. There was another, more pressing thought on his mind. A thought that he could, maybe, do something about. Uncle Harry. How could he help his uncle?

The thought stayed with him all through supper and long into the evening. It was still puzzling him when he put on his special T-shirt, ready for the night ahead, and continued to tickle him when he was tucked up in bed in Uncle Harry's old nursery. *How can I help Uncle Harry? How can I find the truth about the snake?*

Tommy Turner's Tremendous Travels

ᔰ Chapter 11 ᔰ

Myths and Legends

'Who goes there?'

The hushed voice bounced around the space before dispersing into the blackness.

High above, a drip broke the stillness then—*SPLAT*—a large drop landed on Tommy's face. He drew his breath sharply inwards.

'Shush,' hissed the voice. A rustle came from behind, followed by a chilling scrape of metal against stone. Tommy twisted round, squinting into the blackness, willing his eyes to see through the dark. It was no use. The gloom encircled him like a blanket. He reached out with his hand, his fingers groping the ground beneath him. It was icy cold and wet. Jagged edges of granite chafed his skin as he patted the floor, trying to understand where he had arrived. Another drop of water hit him, making his body spasm as it rolled down his neck. Tommy patted again. Further away this time. Once. Twice. The third time, his hand hit nothing but air. He recoiled, afraid of losing his balance.

Gradually, the darkness changed to grey as his eyes adapted to the lack of light. Little by little, shapes emerged around him. *If only I had my torch*, he thought, remembering it was buried beneath his pillow back at Parsons Court.

Suddenly, like a thunderbolt on a summer's day, a hand grasped his mouth. It stifled his involuntary yell, gripping him hard and jerking his head backwards. Seconds later, a cold blade edge dug lightly against his throat. He froze solid. Terrified. The only movement was his pounding heart threatening to explode into a million bloody fragments.

'One sound, and I will have to kill you, understand?' whispered a harsh voice against his cheek. Tommy forced his head to move faintly forward and back in agreement. The hand relaxed slightly against his mouth and the voice whispered again, 'Rise up—slowly.'

He felt a knee jabbing into the small of his back, pushing him forward as he drew himself up.

'Now, walk back. Careful. Do not rush, I will lead. Not a sound, you hear, or we will both be dead.'

It seemed like an eternity as Tommy was half led, half dragged along, slipping on loose stones and jagged edges. Bumping and scraping against the sharp rocks that threatened to chafe his skin raw. And all the time, the hand gripped around his mouth, the steel blade hovering near his throat. His heart was beating at twice its normal speed. *I'm much too young to die*, he thought and wished he could wake up that instant in Uncle Harry's warm, cosy nursery.

By now his eyes had adjusted to the dark, and his terror heightened as he realised he was being dragged along a narrow, high ledge that ran around the side of a vast cavern. The cave looked as though it had been hewn out of the rocks many years ago and then left to decay by itself. Heaps of foul smelling slime clung to the floor. Dank algae and festering fungi protruded from the rock walls, relishing in their soggy surroundings. The smell of oldness invaded his nose. His skin felt bruised and raw from the rough stone edges.

At last, they came to the end of the ledge. The floor widened out into a platform, and they stopped. The hand tightened again around his mouth, and the voice spoke, kindlier this time.

'Do I have your honour that you will not scream?'

Tommy nodded, too fearful to use his voice. The hand pulled away, and Tommy found himself being spun around to face his captor.

The boy was about twenty, tall and manly, his head of dark curls hanging matted and damp around his grimy face. He wore a robe of grey steel belted at the waist by a large leather strap inlayed with copper emblems. His sandals were held fast by leather strips wound tightly around his calves.

'Who are you?' the boy demanded.

'Tommy,' his voice squeaked. 'Tommy Turner.'

'Why are you here, Tommy Turner?' The boy peered closer into Tommy's face. 'From whom were you sent?'

'I'm—not sure really,' Tommy stammered, trying not to stare at the boy's wild eyes. 'I think it was Uncle Harry or maybe Mr Petrovsky.'

The boy opened his mouth to answer, but before he could utter a word, a horrendous screech rose from deep within the cave. The noise vibrated against the walls, echoing again and again up into the vast, cavernous roof.

'Away,' yelled the boy, sprinting off into the darkness. 'Do not look back,' he shouted behind him.

But Tommy's legs were rooted to the floor, paralysed, unable to respond to any thoughts of flight. At the back of the cave, something large and heavy was shuffling ever closer.

Move, please move, he begged. *Now!* A jolt tore through his body, setting every muscle alight with energy. He dashed away as fast as his legs could carry him, keeping the fleeing back of the boy just in sight. Round one tight corner, then another. Spiralling downwards all the time. Knocking against the rough stones, but not caring if he fell, such was his need to escape the horrible sound.

Finally, in the distance, he saw a chink of light. Hope rushed through his body, spurring him onwards. Nearer and nearer he ran. Closer and closer, the light increasing with every step, and then— *BAM!*—he was through the doorway and to safety.

The sun's intensity hit him full in the face, blinding him after the dimness of the cave. He sank to the ground in exhaustion, his breath heavy and laboured, his legs like steel rods. He lay there gulping up the hot, still air, until the dizzy pounding in his head subsided. At last he opened his eyes.

The boy was kneeling over him, whispering. Tommy flinched and drew himself into a tight ball, away from his captor and the memory of the knife blade. The boy chuckled softly.

'Do not alarm yourself, Tommy Turner. Now we are safe, for they come not outside. They come never outside.'

He reached into the folds of his tunic, withdrew a tattered piece of cloth and wiped his sweaty brow. Then he offered it to Tommy, who flinched again and backed away.

'Please, I am sorry. I did not mean to scare you, but you make much noise, and they would all have come out.' His jumbled apology sounded brash and forthright, more like an explanation. Tommy looked up, and the boy smiled.

'I want to hurt you not, by the gods I do not. I had no choice.'

Tommy blinked away an exhausted tear. The trembling started to subside in his exhausted limbs, but he still had no strength left to fight or to run. He was trapped.

The boy's smile widened, and he held out his hand. 'You, me, friends?' he asked.

Tommy blinked again, feeling salty water welling in his eyes. He searched the boy's face for signs of hostility, but there were none. Timidly, he raised his own hand. The boy took it and clasped it firmly.

'Friends,' he repeated with more determination. Then he added, 'Tommy Turner, my newly found friend, I am glad you are here. For I do believe I need your help.'

'My help?' The surprise in Tommy's voice was genuine. What on earth could he do to help this wild looking stranger?

The boy stood and helped Tommy onto his wobbly feet. 'Let us return to camp and have some food, and then I shall tell you everything.'

He turned and started to lead the way down the rocky slope. A few feet later, he stopped and looked back at Tommy, shielding his eyes against the burning sun.

'I forget my manners, friend, for I tell you not my name. I am Perseus, son of Zeus.'

Tommy Turner's Tremendous Travels

✨ Chapter 12 ✨

Perseus' Request

Camp was little more than a large, worn blanket tied haphazardly around the swooping branch of a lone cyprus tree. They were standing high upon a sheer cliff that overhung the turquoise ocean. It stretched evermore away, spanning far beyond the horizon. Way below, white spray sparkled merrily in the glinting sea, its bedazzling dance beckoning Tommy to jump.

Perseus pulled a blackened pot towards them and signalled to Tommy to sit beside him and eat. The food was barely warm. The meat was stringy and tough, each mouthful taking an age to swallow, yet Tommy devoured it heartily, such was his hunger. Perseus sat in silence, tearing off chunks of flesh and stuffing them into his mouth. All the while, he looked out towards the ocean, deep in thought.

When the meal ended Perseus rummaged amongst his possessions and, finding a small hide flask, popped it open and drank with gusto. He passed the bottle to Tommy, who gulped down the sweet, sickly liquor, which spilt out over his chin. It tasted good. Too good. He wanted to lie down and rest. He felt lightheaded from the running, the unforgotten fear and the warmth of the drink seeping through his body. The sun glimmered through the shade of the tree, dappling the ground around him and dancing on his face. He leant his head against the tree trunk and closed his eyes.

'Wake up.'

Tommy jumped at the sound of Perseus's voice, his body rushing back into reality.

'We have no time for sleep,' Perseus continued. 'There is too much to sort out before tonight.'

'Why? What do we have to sort out?' Tommy asked, grumpy at being disturbed.

'First you must agree to help me and then, presuming you will, we must make our plan. We have but one chance. It must be right first time, or we go not at all.'

'Right? Go? I don't understand.' Tommy glared at Perseus. 'What are you talking about? What do you want with me?'

'Do not alarm yourself,' Perseus laughed. 'By the will of the Gods, you are feistier than I thought.' He took another swig from the flask and shifted into a more comfortable position.

'I have been set a challenge,' he started. 'One deadlier and more frightening than that rogue Jason has ever undertaken, and if I am defeated, my mother will forever be the slave of the tyrant, King Polydectes. And have no doubt—he will send his army to kill me, too.'

His dry laugh caught in the back of his throat. 'But Polydectes knows not that I have weapons and tools more lethal than his pathetic army to aid me in my task. Objects the Gods themselves have given me to help me succeed in the challenge. Look, look what Athena gave to me,' he cried, jumping to his feet and throwing back the blanket to reveal a pile of strange looking objects. He sorted swiftly through the pile and then leapt up. He lifted a huge bronze shield triumphantly into the air, tossed his head back and yelled, 'I AM INVINCIBLE!'

As Perseus swung around, the sun's rays stuck upon the shield's centre and its energy shot back into the sky like a jet of molten gold.

He's quite mad, thought Tommy glumly, *but as he's the only friend I have at the moment, I'll have to stick with him until I at least know where I am.* He glanced back towards the pile of treasures, his eyes scanning the array of goodies. Then he saw it.

The blade was half hidden under the blanket, but still it gleamed and twinkled and coaxed him closer. He drew nearer, hypnotised by its magnificence. It made his heart pound. He wanted to touch it, be it, feel the grip of the hilt in his palm. The sword was made of pure gold, encrusted with gems as large as pebbles. Rubies, emeralds and sapphires had been set into an intricate pattern that wove along the sheath's length. In the centre of the handle lay a huge oval diamond bigger than any known to humanity.

Tommy reached out with his right hand and touched the blade. The warmth shot through him, surging up his arm and into his chest. His fingers moved along the sheath and up towards the hilt, tightening around the handle. It seemed to mould into his hand, become part of him, willing him to become part of it. He was at once a great, mighty warrior. Leader of Legions. Slayer of Evil. Champion of Good. The sword's energy raced through his bones, calling out to him. *Now. Take me now.*

Tommy leapt to his feet and pulled the blade free from its sheath, hoisting it high above his head. The swish of the blade whistled in his ears as it flew through the air. He had the strength of a giant, the speed of a leopard, and the valour of a knight.

Perseus's hearty laughter split into Tommy's trance, and Tommy spun round, bearing the sword before him. Perseus was staring wide-eyed in amazement.

'You are a fine swordsman. Perhaps the best I have ever had the pleasure of knowing. Are you, by chance, a soldier by trade?'

Tommy laughed back, relishing the sword's power.

'A soldier. No.'

He swung the sword again, his newfound vigour surging through every pore. Then, bringing the sword to rest, he met Perseus's eye.

'A soldier. No,' he repeated. 'I am an adventurer.'

Perseus stared back at him, impressed.

'An adventurer? No, not an adventurer. You mean a *great* adventurer, and after today, your name will be forever known in history as the man who helped slay Medusa.'

Medusa? Tommy's brain raced through his school lessons. *Medusa?* He knew the name—

Suddenly, it came to him. *Greek mythology. Hair of writhing snakes. Turns men to stone with one glance. Medusa. Lived in a cave. A cave.*

The cave.

The very cave Perseus had found him in.

He thought back to Perseus standing over him outside the cave. *'Now we are safe for they come not outside. They come never outside'.* The shuffling and horrendous screeching, which had chilled him to the bone. Running. Scraping against the rocks. Only they were not rocks. He saw it now. Saw *them* now. The statues. The staring eyes and terrified grimaces of men and beasts. Petrified on the very spot where they had looked upon the face of the Gorgon Medusa.

She was the most feared creature of all time—she and her two immortal sisters, Stheno and Euryale. A single glance from her magical eyes would turn you forever to stone.

And Tommy did not want to be turned into stone. He did not really care much for being a hero, thank you very much. In fact, he would rather be a twelve-year-old boy living in Parsons Court with an annoying brat of a sister. At least then he would be relatively safe. His mind was fizzing with possibilities. Should he run? Refuse to help? Force his body to wake up from this fearful dream?

The words of Mr Petrovsky cut into his thoughts: *'The second lesson is strength. Strength of body and mind to believe you will win, even when you fear the worst. To be able to withstand fright and know you will triumph in the end.'*

This was it then. The second lesson. Mr Petrovsky's wise face rose in his mind. His piercing blue eyes stared at him, willing him to succeed. He thought about taking the Anjulongs back to Yorintown and how scared he had been at first. Scared but excited. He thought about the rush of adrenaline he had felt when the landing disks hit the spaceship, the same adrenaline he felt now with this mighty sword in his hands.

'What say you, Tommy Turner? Have you courage for this adventure?' Perseus lowered his voice, unable to hide his anxiety. 'May I count upon your help?'

Tommy gulped back the lump in his throat and nodded. 'Yes, yes I'll do it. I'll help you, Perseus.'

'You are a brave adventurer and a good friend.' Perseus stepped forward and took Tommy's hand. 'The Gods will not forget you, my good friend. They will keep you safe.'

*

The next few hours rushed by in a haze of excitement. First, Perseus showed Tommy the rest of the treasures he had been given to help him succeed in the task. Then Perseus showed him a pair of winged sandals he had already used to cover the many miles he had travelled to reach the island. Whoever wore these sandals would be able to run like the wind and never be caught. A small leather pouch—a *kibisis* Perseus called it—that would hold any item placed in it, no matter how large or bulky the object. They would use this to carry Medusa's head once she had been slain.

Perseus came to the final object, which looked like a plain piece of jute cloth. Compared with the other items, it did not look worthy of keeping, let alone helping to slay the Gorgon. As Tommy leant back over to re-examine the sandals, he felt a heavy prod in his back. He turned around, brushing it away but felt nothing but air.

'Do you spy me, friend?' Perseus's voice came from behind him.

'Where are you?' Tommy replied, peering into the distance.

Another prod, this time on his side. Tommy jumped to his feet and spun around, again hitting only air.

'Where are you?' he demanded. 'Stop it.'

'Over here!'

Tommy twisted to the left.

'No. Here.'

To the right. 'Stop it, now. Where are you?'

'Up here. Can you see me now?' Perseus was sitting astride the low branch of the cyprus tree, swinging the jute cloth in his hand. 'A fine joke, do you not think, Tommy?' he said, grinning from ear to ear.

'Not really,' retorted Tommy, feeling put out. 'What is that thing anyway?'

"Why it is but the Cap of Hades. Look. Watch.' Perseus placed the hood upon his head and disappeared. 'Here I am!'

Tommy turned around. Perseus was standing a foot away from him, holding the cap.

'Will you try?' He handed Tommy the cap and turned away. 'Conceal yourself, my friend.'

Tommy lifted the hood and placed it over his head. Nothing happened. Everything looked the same as before. How odd, it was as if the cloth was made of invisible thread. He felt a wave of disappointment flicker through him. Why had the hood worked for Perseus and not for him?

'Are you not ready?' Perseus swung round and stared right at him.

Great, thought Tommy.

Then he noticed Perseus's eyes looking not at him but through him, scouring the landscape for a giveaway of his presence. Perseus could not see him and yet Tommy could see everything around him. But of course, it was brilliant. He was invisible.

He let out a cry of pleasure and danced around, lifting the cap off, on, off, on, shouting, 'Here I am. No, I'm not. Here I am. No, I'm not.'

Perseus hooted with laughter, grabbed Athena's shield, and joined in the frenzy until they both fell in a heap to the ground, exhausted but full to the brim with exhilaration.

'And now we plan,' said Perseus, still panting from their exertion. He sat up, crossed his legs, and beckoned for Tommy to do the same.

Tommy's heart quickened, and he felt the hairs on his arms tingle as if an army of ants were speeding along them. He could not back out now. He must not back out now.

'I shall give you the Cap of Hades, for it will shroud you like a thief in the night. I shall take the sandals. They stood me well on my journey here and can be treacherous to use without practice.

Tommy nodded his agreement.

'You will also take the *kibisis*. Do you think you can manage both?'

Tommy nodded again.

'Good.' Perseus smiled. 'I would let you take the sword, but this is my task, and it must be I who slays Medusa.'

Perseus carried on planning, Tommy now and again suggesting possible alternatives to which Perseus readily agreed.

'You have a fine brain, Tommy. Where did you learn such tricks and tactics?'

Tommy thought it best not to mention that the only time he had planned a surprise attack was with Digby last spring, so he sat quietly, trying to look as heroic as possible.

The main problem was how to creep up on the Gorgons without the sisters seeing them. They could not very well keep their eyes shut and go stumbling about in the darkness, but just one unconscious glance and they would be forever turned to stone.

Tommy racked his brain for an answer. What could they use to shield themselves from the three sisters? He looked out towards the ocean and saw the sun dancing over the waves. Reflecting back at him. Glinting like a spotlight in a mirror. A mirror—that was it!

'The shield, Perseus. We can use the shield Athena gave you. If we keep our eyes glued to the shield, it will show us Medusa's reflection. Then we can see her without looking at her.'

'Masterly, my friend. Quite masterly. By the Gods, was I lucky to have met you,' said Perseus eagerly. 'Well, I think our plan is complete. Once more through it, I think, so we are clear on every detail.'

Tommy Turner's Tremendous Travels

⚜ Chapter 13 ⚜

The Battle of the Gorgons

Tommy sat at the edge of the cliff, watching the ocean turn crimson as the sun sank beyond the horizon. Earlier, while Perseus had been taking a nap, he had managed to find a narrow, windy, overgrown path and scramble down to the beach below to take a dip in the cool waters. The spray from the waves, which had seemed so small from the cliff top, splashed over his head as he bounded through it. The sea tasted salty on his lips.

When his fingers had turned wrinkly from the water, he sat on the beach, drying in the sun and contemplating the task ahead of him.

He was not exactly nervous. In fact, he felt an overwhelming calmness about him, as though he knew already he would be safe. Protected. Yes, that was the word. Held by an invisible thread, which led back to his old life. His mind wandered to Sally and his new school. Normally, the mere thought of them would make his hands clench in anger. But now, everything seemed so tiny and far away. How unimportant it all was. He thought about Digby and the gang; what they would have done to be with him right now on a real adventure.

He resolved there and then that, when he got back home, he would try not to let things upset him anymore. He would find his own way at school. He would make new friends. He would even try not to allow his mum's clear favouritism of Sally get him down. And all the while, Mr Petrovsky would be there to help and advise him and to listen to Tommy's strange tales of Anjulongs and Gorgons and whatever else there might be.

Now, sitting on the cliff edge in the dusky warmth of the evening, Tommy felt as though his stomach were full of frogs. His body buzzed with expectation. He felt more alive than ever before in his short, ordinary life. Ready to spring into action at the faintest noise.

He heard Perseus calling and turned around. Perseus was coming towards him clasping their weapons in his hands.

'It's time, my friend, it's time.'

*

The slope up to the cave was tough going, full of loose stones that slipped beneath Tommy's feet, leaving clouds of dust in their wake. But finally, they reached the top, both out of breath and panting from the climb. Straight ahead, the mouth of the cave yawned, its jagged rocks resembling broken, rotten teeth. Tommy could feel his heart pumping with anticipation of what lay inside. He patted the small dagger Perseus had given him for safety, which was tied securely to his belt alongside the *kibisis*.

Perseus turned to him with some final instructions.

'We shall go partway into the cave before I put on the sandals and you the Cap of Hades. That way we can keep together and know where the other is standing. I shall lead, but you must keep close behind. They always sleep at the back of the cave, so we have nothing to fear. Be alert. Be ready to run or to fight and remember, whatever you do, keep looking into the shield.'

Without another moment's hesitation they stepped into the cave.

At once, the cold stale air wrapped itself around Tommy, chilling his very soul. He squinted in the darkness, blinking until the greyness became recognisable objects. His breath caught in his throat at the sight of the silent, algae-ridden figures staring into the abyss with the same horrified look on their stony faces. He reached out and touched one; feeling its cold, damp lifelessness.

On and on they marched. Every few feet, the air grew cooler and the dampness clung to Tommy's skin. Millennia old stalagmites and stalactites clung tight to the cave walls. They had been growing endlessly, drip by drip, ever since time began. Up and up the two intrepid adventurers climbed, until they reached the very slope they had met upon earlier that day.

At last, Perseus stopped and turned to Tommy. His face looked white and drawn, and he seemed much older than Tommy remembered him.

'Just around the corner is where the Gorgons sleep,' he whispered. 'Put on the Cap and remember, once you do, I shall know not where you are. You must stay with me. Once I have slain Medusa, I will wait until you grab her head, and then I will run like the wind out of here. You will have to make your own way out, but you can take your time. They will not be able to see you. And Tommy, whatever you do, do not look at her head before you put it in the *kibisis.*'

He bent down and swiftly changed into the winged sandals. Tommy saw their energy shooting up into Perseus's body as he placed them on his feet, their magic entwining and enchanting every fibre of his body. Tommy took the Cap of Hades and placed it over his head.

'Are you ready, my friend?' whispered Perseus.

Tommy nodded his agreement; then realising Perseus could not see him anymore, whispered back, 'Yes, I'm ready.'

'Then may the power of Zeus himself be with us,' murmured Perseus as he vanished around the corner.

Scared to lose his companion so soon, Tommy hastened onwards. As he turned the corner, his eyes fell for a split second on the vast cavern spreading out below him. He spun away, fearful of being petrified, but his mind had already registered the eerie scene. And what he had witnessed chilled him to the very marrow.

The three sisters were huddled together in their makeshift bed. It resembled a huge matted nest, which had been made from decaying twigs and branches. Scattered around the edge of the nest lay discarded bones and rotting pieces of flesh, the remains of the prey on which they gorged themselves. Tommy's stomach heaved, and his knees wobbled as the smell of putrid meat seeped into his nostrils. Many of the bones looked remarkably large, and Tommy wondered rather shakily if they were the remains of some poor unfortunate hunters who had taken refuge in the cave during a storm and whom the sisters had crept up upon while they were sleeping. He brushed the thought away, praying he would not come to the same dreadful end.

In the centre of the nest lay the Gorgons. Asleep, thankfully. Their hideousness was terrifying. One could vaguely see they had once been human, but their transformation was as wicked as it had been complete. From their faces grew huge tusks like those of a boar, the ends so pointed and sharp that one stab would kill a person instantly.

Giant lizard scales, of the size you would expect to see upon a dragon, covered their whole body from the neck down. Each scale looked as hard as granite, as knobbly as a clamshell.

Wrapped around each body was a pair of enormous, golden wings. Not wondrous, magnificent angel wings, but tatty, torn protrusions that looked as if they had just this minute returned from a weeklong battle.

The sisters' hands, much larger than human hands, were made from bronze. Each fingernail was razor-sharp, like a talon, ready to rip apart anyone who dared approach them.

But the worst, the absolute horror of their appearance, was the multitude of snakes slithering and sliming and clinging around their faces, hissing and rearing up in an endless seething mass. Some were so large they reached the full length of the Gorgons' bodies. Some were as thick as a child's arm. Some of the snakes spat lime green phlegm that looked like the deadliest of poisons. And as the sisters lay slumbering, these serpents slithered endlessly in their hypnotic dance, luring their prey with luminous, yellow, unblinking eyes.

As Tommy turned back, he saw Perseus making his way over some high rocks at the side of the cave. In his hurry to catch up, Tommy slipped amongst the rocks. Dust and pebbles scattered down onto the cave floor. At once, a hundred snakeheads twisted towards the noise, their evil eyes peering in his direction. Some of the larger creatures shot through the air until they came to within inches of Tommy and he could see their fangs oozing with venom.

He clasped the side of the rock on which he was perched and froze. His heart pounded like a pneumatic drill in his chest, and he felt sure the noise would echo throughout the cavern. The snakes twisted and slithered in the air, hissing and spitting as they recoiled, ready to spring again when they had found their prey. But the magic Cap of Hades was doing its job, and they searched in vain; Tommy was as invisible as a speck of gold upon the cave floor. After what seemed like an eternity, the serpents withdrew to the nest.

Once Tommy's heartbeat had subsided, he silently inched his way onwards towards Perseus. As he got near, Tommy reached out and tapped Perseus twice, keeping his hand resting on his friend's shoulder. This was the sign they had agreed upon if Tommy needed to get Perseus's attention. Perseus tapped the invisible hand three times. *Are you alright?* Tommy tapped again once. *Yes, fine.* He wished he could say, 'Not really,' but they had not worked out a sign for that. The older boy turned back, placed his finger on his lips to keep Tommy silent and beckoned him onwards.

For the next five minutes, they moved like ghosts, edging noiselessly over the rocks until at last they were directly above the back of the Gorgons' nest. Perseus beckoned again to Tommy and slipped through a gap in the rocks. Tommy followed.

He found himself in a tight crevice barely big enough for the two of them but at least out of sight of the snakes. He reached up and removed the cap, so Perseus could see him.

'What happened? It seems you had a shave of the closest kind,' whispered Perseus.

'You're telling me,' said Tommy breathlessly. 'Especially when that huge red snake lunged at me. I thought it was going to get me. I can't tell you how scared I was at first, because I'd forgotten I was invisible to them.'

'No harm done, thank the Gods.' Perseus laughed silently, then his face took on a more serious look. 'We are here now, Tommy. Just one final step, and our task will be over. Do you remember the plans down to every last detail? Good! Are you ready to be a hero? Good! Here we go then!'

With one bound, he sprang out of the crevice and, swinging his sword high above his head, jumped over the rock face and into the Gorgons' bed. Seconds later, Tommy was flying through the air, his eyes shut tightly, his hand grasping the *kibisis*. He found himself falling down, down, down into the nest below. He hit the floor and immediately scrambled to his feet as Perseus yelled, 'HERE!'

Locating the noise in a breath, Tommy swung round to face Perseus. He opened his eyes. Perseus was already on his feet, staring intently into the huge shield. Tommy fixed his gaze onto the same spot. His scream echoed around the rocks as the terrifying vision reflected back.

The Gorgons were stirring, furious at such an abrupt and unpleasant rousing. They were screeching and howling and waving their arms blindly in the air as they tried to arise from their deep slumber. But as their huge lumbering bodies rolled backwards and forward, Tommy suddenly understood what was happening. The sisters were quarrelling. They jabbed and slapped one another in order to find which of them was to blame for the disturbance. And they were so busy with the entire affair, this appalling hullabaloo, they had not yet seen the real reason for their awakening.

Now was their chance. They had to attack this instant.

'Perseus, strike now!' yelled Tommy as loudly as his lungs would allow him.

Perseus sprang into action, raised his golden sword high into the air, and swung it downwards with all his strength. The sword whooshed through the air and—*THWACK*—it sliced straight through Medusa's neck like a newly sharpened guillotine. As it struck, she let out a single ear-piercing scream, which reverberated endlessly away through the cavern. Her head flew through the air and landed a few feet from Tommy, splattering him with blood. Her snake hair lay tangled in a mass of coils, their eyes already glazed with the look of death.

The other sisters, by this time, had stopped their quarrel and, howling like wolves caught in a trap, turned to face the two boys. They opened their enormous wings and started shaking them to and fro, whipping them through the air. Tommy knew one blow from

their wings would mean certain death, so he flung himself to the ground and scrambled away. Their snake hair was writhing to and fro, preparing for battle, darting back and forth with a life of its own. They crouched low on their scaly legs, ready to spring forward and attack their assailants. Tommy trembled with fear. He felt hopeless against these great monsters. The wind from their wings cut into his back with the force of a tornado. Their hot breath mingled with the cold chill of terror that ran down his spine.

'Quick—her head,' shouted Perseus. 'No time to—'

At that moment, one of the sisters leapt forward in a single bound and reached for the head herself. Tommy hurled himself backwards and landed between her legs, keeping his eyes trained on the shield Perseus held firmly before him. He threw his arm out, stretching as far as he could and groped madly about until his hand clasped the thick body of a snake. Gripping with all his might, Tommy swung the head back through the Gorgon's legs and stuffed it straight into the *kibisis*. The tiny pouch, which looked as though it could carry no more than a few coins, swallowed the gigantic head whole until it disappeared from sight.

'Run, Perseus. Run!' yelled Tommy, scrambling to the side of the nest and away from the Gorgon.

Perseus took one last look into the shield, flung it to the ground, and then in a great leap, sprang up onto the ledge from which they had originally jumped.

'See you at camp, Tommy Turner,' he cried as he bounded over the rocks. In a blink of an eye, he was gone

Meanwhile, the sisters were searching desperately for their sister's head. They patted about in the bedding, crying and moaning with pain and bewilderment, oblivious to everything else going on around them. They did not hear Tommy yelling or see Perseus jump onto the ledge. They did not see the shield where it lay cast aside. All they wanted was their sister's head. But at the very last second as Perseus disappeared around the corner, one of the sisters swung her head towards him and spied him fleeing away. She gave a thunderous bellow and leapt into the air in pursuit. Her great wings flapped around her as she half flew, half ran after him. The second sister, seeing her sibling's fury, chased after her.

Tommy was at last alone. Was at last safe. For the time being, at least.

✎ Chapter 14 ✎

Escape From the Gorgons

The first thing Tommy did was to take a deep breath in order to calm down and collect his thoughts. The cave sounded eerily quiet after the racket of the last few minutes, although he could still hear the cries of the sisters receding into the distance. *I wonder what's happened to Perseus,* he thought. *Have the winged sandals saved him? Has he made it to the cave's entrance in time? Or is he now a stone replica of himself or, worse still, a Gorgon morsel?* He shivered at the idea of his friend's fate, then quickly brushed it away. Now was not the time to think these horrible thoughts. He too had to find his own way out of the cave and to safety. *I really ought to be making a move right now*, he thought.

He reached down and felt the *kibisis*. The bulge inside the pouch was no larger or heavier than a walnut. *How can her head have gotten so small*, he thought. *Can it really be inside the bag?* Gingerly, he poked his hand inside just to make sure. His fingers at once squelched into the spongy, warm flesh, and he withdrew them in haste, shuddering at the thought of what lay within. He tied the *kibisis* tightly and checked it was still held securely by his belt.

A minute passed and then another, and still Tommy sat. He knew he should move but felt quite unable. He thought he should at least try and move his legs, but it all seemed so much of an effort. He actually felt quite cosy in all this giant bedding and, he said to himself, it was probably a good idea to rest for a while before trying to climb back along the rocks. He felt as though he was being lulled into a gentle doze.

That would be nice, he thought, *forty winks before I get going,* and he laid his head against the side of the nest. *No one can see me, so I'll be quite safe for a while.* His eyelids started to droop. *I'll just sneak away when those horrid creatures return*, he yawned.

The magic nest started to weave its deadly charm, soothing Tommy into a stupor of complete and utter relaxation. Its heavy drug crept into his skin and tiptoed through his veins, like a skilful, silent burglar. Many men and beasts had found their end this way. Tommy had been right about the bones he had seen scattered around the nest.

He was settling into a lovely, welcoming slumber when he became aware of a strange, ripping noise coming from the middle of the nest. It sounded like a gigantic tree in the final stages of being felled, creaking and groaning as it plunged to the ground. It was not a pleasant noise. In fact, it was quite unnerving and not at all the sort of thing you want to hear when you are trying to have a snooze. The sound changed now to a squelching, sucking noise, like something being pulled out of thick, gooey mud. Louder and louder it grew, *squelch, suck, squelch*. Tommy shook the sleep from his body and turned to face the noise. This time, he did not have to worry about looking at the Gorgon's headless body, as he knew only her eyes could harm him.

What he saw was the strangest, most surprising, unpleasantly compelling thing he had ever seen in his life. For out of Medusa's severed neck a slimy bulge appeared, and it seemed to be growing larger by the second. Tommy stared, mesmerised, as the thing heaved and swelled and pushed its way forward, until at last he was able to distinguish a shape amongst the bloody tendons. It was the shape of a head. But it was not a human head Tommy was staring at. It was, in fact, the head of a foal. The nose and ears were already visible, and its long neck was starting to emerge. All of a sudden, it opened its mouth and gave a little whinny, as if to say hello. Pretty soon the whole neck had come into view, then the front hooves and body. It struggled and heaved, forcing its way out, until finally the back legs and tail came into sight and the little creature slid with a plop onto the bedding. It did look forlorn, lying there covered in blood and blinking hard with its huge brown eyes.

Tommy eyes were also as big and bulgy as over-blown balloons. He pinched himself a couple of times to make sure he had not been transported into another different world within an already different world—a world where dead monsters gave birth to farmyard animals from the place where their head used to be—*EWWWW YUCK!!!*

After a minute or so, the foal tried to clamber to its feet. It staggered onto its back legs, which trembled for a second or two and then slid out from under its weak body and *PLONK*, the foal tumbled back to the ground. It tried again and again until at last its back legs were firm on the floor and then pushed up with its front legs until finally it was standing upright, its spindly legs spreading awkwardly in every direction. It stayed frozen to the spot, unable to move for fear of collapsing yet again. Its tiny heart was beating like a sewing machine stitching at full pelt, its whimsical eyes drawing Tommy into the depth of its soul.

'Poor little thing,' he said out loud to himself, and picking up some leaves from the nest, he crept over and started to wipe the blood off the creature.

'You don't have anyone to help you into the world, do you? But don't worry, I shall do my best,' he added, and the foal nuzzled softly against his neck.

He wiped down its neck and along its back, noticing two unsightly lumps protruding from its withers. As he dabbed them clean, he realised in horror that the foal's skin was falling away in his hands.

He shrank back, sickened by what he had done, but it seemed not to have hurt the animal. Not in the slightest. In fact, the foal moved toward him and started rubbing against him. Pretty soon all the skin had disappeared, and in its place two golden cherub wings sprang forth. The foal gave a long whinny and frolicked around Tommy, clearly delighted by its new appendages.

'You're a magical horse, are you?' said Tommy, spinning round to catch the foal. 'Well, hold still a minute, and let me finish cleaning you. Then we shall have to think what to do with you.'

He knelt and wiped the foal's legs. It was an endless job. As soon as he thought he had finished one leg, it appeared to have grown larger and stronger and there was even more to clean. He looked up at the foal's body. It too was growing and at such a pace it was already twice the size it had been a moment ago. Its shoulders grew broad and muscular, its nose grew wide and graceful and its tiny wings swelled and spread until they were strong and powerful.

Tommy stared at the beauty of this wild, majestic creature standing before him.

'Pegasus,' he murmured in wonderment.

The horse stepped towards him and, pushing up Tommy's head, licked him hard on the face.

'Ugh, get off,' said Tommy, for nobody likes to be licked in the face by a horse, even one as great as Pegasus. Then, realising what had happened, he added, 'So you can see me, can you?'

The horse licked him again and nudged him sideways.

'Ugh, stop that,' Tommy demanded. The horse nudged him again, this time with more force. 'I said stop th—'

Pegasus reared up in front of him, his nostrils flaring. Then, letting out the biggest snort, he fell to the ground and kicked his legs madly about him, rolling on his back with sheer abandonment.

'This is your idea of a joke, is it, Pegasus?' said Tommy, laughing at the sight of the huge animal. Pegasus took one last roll, righted himself and stared at Tommy. Then, with one bound, he was at Tommy's side, nipping gently at his tunic.

'Pegasus, I'm so glad you're here,' cried Tommy. He flung his arms around the horse's neck, breathing in the warm, horsey scent of his body.

In his excitement, Tommy had forgotten all about Gorgons, escaping the nest and finding safety, but at that moment, two simultaneous sounds sent him spiralling back to reality.

From Medusa's still body came the same squelching, sucking noises as before. Another shape was appearing from the severed neck. Its silhouette towered above the nest, dwarfing the shape of the foal that had appeared earlier. But his real fear came from the other sound. The screeching and scraping that sprang from within the cave told Tommy the sisters were on their way back to the nest. They could be here at any moment.

Quick as a flash, he spun to face Pegasus.

'We're in danger,' he yelled. 'We must escape right now, or all will be lost!'

Pegasus whinnied and clambered down onto his front legs. Tommy tore over to where Perseus had earlier cast the shield aside. He grabbed it and, with a flying leap, jumped astride Pegasus. Pegasus sprang into action. He cleared the nest with a single bound, spread his huge wings in full glory and soared high into the air.

'Fly, Pegasus, fly!' shouted Tommy, clinging on for dear life. He had never sat astride a horse before, let alone flown one. 'Don't look down, or all will be lost,' he added, his voice muffled amid Pegasus's wild mane.

Up and up they soared, dashing past giant stalactites that hung suspended from the towering roof, Tommy ducking this way and that to avoid the sharp edges. Pegasus flew with such speed the cold cave air stung Tommy's face.

Leaning slightly to one side, he took the shield and positioned it so he had a clear view of the ground below. The sisters were jumping in the air with rage, shaking their fists at the fleeing horse and screaming chants, which disappeared in echoes around the cave. Craning his neck even more, Tommy could see a huge, grotesque shape lying at the back of the nest. It was the second beast that had appeared from Medusa's dead body. It was so unlike Pegasus that had Tommy not witnessed its birth, he would never have imagined it could have come from the same body.

It was of human form but five times larger than Tommy had ever seen before. Its legs were as thick as oak trees, its hair as matted as ivy. It cried like a new-born baby, but the noise sounded more like the screech of a raptor. It was a giant, born from all the worst parts of Medusa. The twin of Pegasus. The dark to Pegasus's light. And in its right hand lay a copy of the golden sword with which Perseus had slain the Gorgon Medusa.

Pegasus sped through the cave, weaving around the obstacles that lay in his path. His great wings whipped through the air as Tommy clung on with all his might.

'Watch out,' he cried suddenly, throwing himself against the horse's body. An enormous stalactite was hurtling through the air at them. Pegasus veered to the right, but the stalactite tore into Tommy's arm on its descent to the floor below. The pain was fearful and immediate. It burnt into his flesh. Blood scattered into the air below them and onto Pegasus's flanks. Tommy cried out in terror as the pain seared through his body, which was already numb with fear.

He felt dizzy, weak. His remaining strength drained from his tired limbs. All he could do was cling on to Pegasus and pray not to fall hundreds of feet to his death. The hot, sticky blood gushed from his wound, soaking his leg. His arm hung limply at his side.

Slowly, Pegasus descended from the roof of the cave. Down and down he flew, as gently as possible. On and on he soared until finally, just as Tommy felt he could hold on no longer, they reached the cave's entrance.

The fresh night air hit Tommy full in the face. It was the most wonderful fresh air he had ever tasted, and feebly he gulped some in. Pegasus alighted on the gravelly path at the cave's opening and stood there, tail swishing and nostrils flaring, as he too breathed in the much-needed air.

'Camp below,' murmured Tommy, too weak to move. He lay along Pegasus's back, still clutching the shield in his good hand. The horse softly whinnied his understanding and set off down the path, picking his way through the loose stones.

As they neared camp, Tommy recognised through half-closed eyes the shape of Perseus silhouetted by the flames of the fire. Two other figures were sitting with him. One of the strangers looked up and spotted the horse coming towards them. He beckoned to the others, and all three jumped to their feet and rushed over.

Tommy could feel himself being lifted from the horse and gently carried back to camp. His head felt hot and tight as if it were being squeezed through a mangle, yet his body was trembling with cold. The heavy shield was taken from him. Voices whispered urgently to each other. 'Be gentle with him.' 'Look, he is hurt badly.' 'Go, fetch some water.'

He forced his eyes open a fraction and saw, kneeling before him, the most beautiful woman he had ever seen in his life. Her grey eyes were soft with tears as she soothed his burning forehead. Her anxious mutterings pulsated through his head, then he heard Perseus's fearful voice replying. What was that he said? Athena? He glanced again at the noble woman attending him. Athena. The goddess of wisdom, courage and strength. The goddess of war. Terrifying, powerful Athena. And yet Tommy felt an overwhelming calm in her presence.

The other stranger knelt beside her and whispered in her ear. Athena reached over and quickly untied the *kibisis* from Tommy's belt. He had forgotten all about the pouch and its contents, but suddenly the horror of the past few hours came flooding back to him. He cried out, tossing and turning, trying to tell them of his escape from the sisters, the baby giant, the birth of Pegasus. But his words were lost in a jumble of incoherence. They babbled forth without meaning.

'Great speed, Athena,' urged the stranger. 'He must partake of the blood, if we are to revive him.'

'By the Gods, have patience, Hermes,' said Athena, reaching inside the *kibisis* and feeling around.

'Well, is it there?' asked Hermes.

'So it is,' replied Athena.

'Then break off a piece of her hair and let him drink the blood. Take care it is from her right side, for the left will poison him immediately.'

Tommy felt his mouth being forced open and the sticky trickle of thick, warm liquid dripping into his mouth. Gorgon's blood. He thought he might retch. He had to stop them. Had to fight against it. With his last strength he reached for the snake hair. He grabbed it from Athena's hand and collapsed back on to the hard ground.

His head was spinning too fast. His heart had got stuck mid-pump. He felt himself sinking into the earth, slowly at first but gradually picking up speed. The last thing he felt was Pegasus's warm breath and soft nose nuzzling his face as Perseus's cries faded into the distance.

❧ Chapter 15 ❦

Lunch With the Higgins Twins

A cockerel was crowing in the far distance, proudly proclaiming the day's arrival to the neighbourhood and beyond. Down below, the muffled chime of the hall clock rang the ninth hour of the day. The sounds were ones he had heard a hundred times before, but still Tommy wondered if he was dreaming them.

His eyes felt as though they had been super-glued together, but eventually, like prising the lid of a sticky treacle jar, he forced them open. At the far end of the room, a ray of sunlight poured in through a chink in the curtains, dust fairies dancing in its golden beam.

He tilted his head a fraction to the right and took in the familiar surroundings of Uncle Harry's nursery: the faded yellow wallpaper, the threadbare Persian carpet, the duck-down quilt with its faint smell of mothballs.

Reassured, he closed his eyes again, and Athena's face came flooding into view. *Be gentle with him. Look, he is hurt badly.* He could feel her tenderness as she stroked his hair.

The sound of footsteps on the second-floor landing told him his parents were up. Soon they would be calling him for breakfast.

He felt the warm breath of Pegasus, his velvet nose nuzzling the nape of his neck. Far away, a faint whinny rang in his ears like a familiar ghost. Pegasus. If only Tommy could see him one last time. Feel the warmth of his body. Smell his wonderful horsey scent.

The hall clock struck its quarter, and the aroma of bacon wafted up to the nursery and settled in Tommy's nose. His stomach gurgled in response. Breakfast. Time to get up.

He sat up, and at once a throbbing pain shot through his body, making him wince in agony. His arm was red hot. It felt as if a dozen woodpeckers had been using it to search for grubs. He looked down and saw that his arm was covered with dried blood. But worse still, there was a large open gash on the upper part, which looked like it was starting to decompose. He could already smell the odour of rotting flesh.

Tommy had to sort this out right now before the wound got worse. But what could he do? Who could he go to? There was no way he could tell his parents.

Maybe Uncle Harry? But what would he say? 'Can you help me, Uncle Harry? I was off fighting the Gorgons last night and got hurt. Think it might be infected.' No, that was ridiculous. The only person who would understand was Mr Petrovsky, and he was miles away. His eyes skimmed the room searching for something, *anything* he could use to fight the infection. Mr Petrovsky would know what to use. What would he say if he were here? Tommy's brain was throbbing as hard as his arm—

That's it! The flask. What about the flask Mr Peeves-Withers gave me up in Yorintown. Would that help?

He clambered out of bed, flinching in agony as he moved, and hurried over to his bag. Tucked away at the bottom lay Mr Petrovsky's old box. Tommy removed the key from around his neck and undid the rusty lock. He took out the flask and, taking care not to spill any, popped open the stopper and took a couple of sips.

The bitter liquid left an acidic trail on the back of his tongue, the taste so different to the one he remembered from Yorintown. He shuddered and glanced at the laceration on his arm. It had turned a sort of icky green colour; globules of yellow pus oozed like melted cheese from its centre. He peered closer; was that a maggot wriggling to the surface? The liquid was clearly not working; his arm was worsening. Panic smacked him at full force. Gangrene. He had read about it at school. He would have to chop his arm off. What could he use? Think. Think. Maybe it was already too late. Poison was already pumping through his blood vessels, rushing towards his heart. Tommy looked again at the flask. It had to work. It was his only chance.

This time, he poured a couple of drops onto his arm. In a flash, his wound started stinging with such ferocity it made his eyes fill with tears. The pain was unbearable. It shot through his body in fiery spasms. Tommy clutched his arm and prayed for it to stop.

Just as suddenly as it had started, the pain subsided into an aching numbness. And then a miracle happened.

Before his very eyes, the wound started to close until it had vanished into the contours of his skin. The angry redness of the infection faded into normality, and one by one his freckles reappeared. Finally, it was gone.

Tommy touched his arm. It felt smooth and new. All that was left was the tiniest trace of a scar, invisible to everyone except Tommy. He, on the other hand, would remember it always and forever be reminded of the day he fought Medusa and nearly died.

A gong resounded throughout the house, announcing breakfast time. *Bang* went the door opposite his room as Sally came hurtling out of her room, rapping on Tommy's door as she passed.

'Better get down quick, stupid, or I'll eat all the food,' she shouted.

Tommy took a deep breath. *Nothing is going to upset me today. Not Sally, not Mum, no one.*

'Tell Mum, I'll just be two minutes,' he called back cheerfully. Then he smiled to himself. *No, nothing is going to upset me today. For I, Tommy Turner, am a mythical Greek hero. Ready to do battle with the fiercest, most dangerous creatures in the world.*

And with that, he hurried off to get dressed.

It was after Tommy had flung on his clothes from the day before and was hunting under the bed for his shoes that he saw it. Uncle Harry's fossilised snake. But surely that was impossible. He had clearly seen Uncle Harry putting it in the safe yesterday. He pulled it out and peered closely.

Was it Uncle Harry's fossil? It looked almost identical, but on closer examination it was smaller and had a reddish tinge.

A memory flashed through his head. Hermes.

Break off a piece of her hair and let him drink the blood. Take care it is from her right side, for the left will poison him immediately.

Then another memory rushed by.

Athena pouring the sweet, sickly blood into his mouth. Him trying to stop her.

What if it's the snake I grabbed from Athena, he thought. *It's possible it could be. In fact, it must be the snake. It's the only explanation.*

Suddenly, it dawned on him. Uncle Harry's fossil. It had also come from Medusa's head. The fossil in the museum as well. Not that anyone would ever be able to prove it. But at least it meant Uncle Harry had discovered something so valuable and precious he would never again have to worry about losing Meadowhill Grange.

Tommy would be the only person in the world to know the real truth. Him and Mr Petrovsky, of course. But with school and homework and everything, it would be ages before he could see Mr Petrovsky again. Too long, in fact. He had so much to tell him. So many questions to ask and so many answers to find.

I'll not wear the T-shirt again until I've told Mr Petrovsky everything, he decided and yawned out loud. *Anyway, I really need to get a good night's sleep for once.*

*

Monday morning dawned and with it another day at High Brooms, which in turn meant another meeting with the Higgins Twins. Tommy's tummy woke up in knots. It made him realise he still had a lot to do before he could call himself a real hero. *But,* he thought with relief, *at least the Twins do not have giant tusks and snake hair.*

Not everything was going to be bad that day, however. In the afternoon they had football practice with Mr Adams, and today he would be picking the year's team. Tommy was pretty sure he would get a place. Maybe even captain if he played really well.

The morning turned out to be quite uneventful, and Tommy had almost forgotten about Shaun and Stu's threats. But at lunchtime, as he was waiting at the foot of the stairs in the long canteen queue, he was reminded in an all too familiar way.

'Oy, grease head, have a nice weekend, did ya?'

Tommy felt a lump rise in his throat as Shaun came slithering up behind him, cracking his knuckles for emphasis. The other boys in the queue tried to melt into the surrounding walls.

'Hoped we'd bump into you. Wanted to see if you'd done anything about our little conversation.'

'Oh, hi Shaun,' gulped Tommy, glancing around for an escape route.

'What Shaun really means,' growled Stu, appearing at the top of the stairs and blocking Tommy's only means of escape, 'is 'ave you got our money?'

'Well, it's interesting you should say that,' replied Tommy, trying to stall as his mind reeled with escape plans. How was he going to get out of this one?

Stu headed down the stairs until he was only three steps above Tommy. The queue moved steadily upwards towards the odour of mashed potatoes and cabbage. The boys' whispers grew louder as the message ran through the queue, 'Fight starting on lower ground.' All around, faces stared in anticipation. Yet Tommy was oblivious to everything except the pounding of his heart, the crashing between his ears. His body coiled like a spring about to be released.

'What d'you mean "interesting"?' sneered Shaun.

'You trying to be funny or what?' added Stu, his right hand tightening into a fist.

The queue moved up a stair.

'Funny. No.' Anger rose in Tommy's body. Who were these two punks anyway! 'It's just that I don't like threats, and you two are getting in my face,' he hissed, shocking himself as much as the boys around him.

The whispers in the queue started to change. Tommy was standing up to the Higgins Twins. 'And what's more,' growled Tommy, his strength building into a crescendo. 'You've picked the wrong guy to fight this time.'

Surprise swept across Stu's face. Then his eyes narrowed, and his lip curled upwards.

'So, you wanna fight, do you?' he sneered. 'Come on then. Let's see how quick I can turn you into dog food.'

The queue moved up another step. Tommy was now one stair away from Stu. He could see the tendons on Stu's neck tensing as his eyes narrowed in anger.

'Go on, Stu,' called Shaun from behind. 'Show him who's boss round here.'

'Fight. Fight. Fight. Turner. Turner. Turner.' The soft chants rose up around them, echoing up the dingy narrow stairway. Some of the smaller boys clambered to get out of the way. Tommy drew himself into a knot, waiting to pounce or duck, to react to whatever came his way. Stu's arm drew back, ready to come crashing down on his head. Any second now.

The queue moved quickly up. Two steps this time. Tommy sprang forward, seizing the opportunity to get above Stu before he realised what was happening.

'Watch out!' shouted Shaun to his brother.

But it was too late. Tommy's right foot landed squarely on Stu's behind, sending him crashing down the stairs towards Shaun, who squealed like a pig. Stu slammed into Shaun, and the two brothers tumbled down the few steps and landed in a heap at the bottom, their legs and arms sticking out of the pile as if they were one giant spider. Their cries of 'HELP!' and 'OOWWAH!' were muffled by the hoots of laughter reverberating along the queue.

But now, Tommy had to escape. Quick as a flash he tore up the stairs. He rounded the corner and flew straight into Mr Philips, who had come to see what all racket was about.

Mr Philips grabbed him by the ear and held him tight. The queue was silent, waiting to see what would happen next. Down below, the Higgins Twins groaned with indignation, their pride hurt much more than their bodies.

'What's going on, Turner?' demanded Mr Philips.

Tommy gulped. Out of one mess, straight into another.

'I just want to see what's for lunch today, sir,' he lied, trying to look as innocent as possible.

'That's right, sir,' piped up one of the boys in the queue. 'Tommy didn't do anything.'

Some of the other boys muttered their agreement.

'Is that true, Scott?' Mr Philips asked another boy.

'Yes, sir. Higgins tripped on the stairs and fell on top of his brother.'

'He did, sir. Honestly,' said another.

Tommy glanced at the boys' faces: expectant, encouraging, acknowledging. Wanting to help him, sticking up for him, finally accepting him.

119

Mr Philips let go of Tommy's ear. 'Hmmm, sounds a bit fishy to me,' he barked. 'You can go for now, Turner. But be clear, I'll be watching you from now on.

'Yes, sir, of course. Thank you, sir,' said Tommy, rubbing his throbbing earlobe.

Mr Philips descended the stairs to clear up the mess below, glancing round once to make sure Tommy was behaving himself. The queue continued slowly up the stairs as order was restored.

'Here, Tommy, you can go in front of me, if you like,' said Simon Gillett, his classmate. Simon patted him on the shoulder, adding, 'Amazing. I've never seen anyone stand up to the Twins before.'

But after what had just occurred, Tommy did not think his stomach could hold even a mouthful of lunch. Okay, so he could demolish terrifying mythical creatures, but what would happen next when the Higgins Twins caught up with him?

'Thanks, Simon, but I think I'd better give it a miss this time,' he replied, gesturing toward the foot of the stairs.

'Don't worry about them. Just give us a shout if things get a bit rough, Okay? We like a challenge, don't we lads,' said Simon, punching the air with his fists.

The other boys nodded in agreement.

'By the way,' Simon continued, 'we're going out to the football pitch after lunch to practise before the game this afternoon, if you'd like to come.'

'Would I like to come? That would be awesome—thanks.'

'There you go, then. See you there in half an hour.'

'Wicked, Simon. See you all later.'

Tommy sped off around the corner, a grin spreading into the corners of his mouth. Okay, he would have to face the Higgins Twins again, but maybe, just maybe, he had some allies after all.

❧ Chapter 16 ❧

Football Results

Tuesday passed at a snail's pace. Tommy had not heard a murmur from Shaun and Stu Higgins since his victory. Rumour had it that they were both holed up in sickbay, Stu with a dislocated shoulder blade and Shaun with a bout of flu. Skiveitus would probably be a more appropriate name for it. The whole school seemed to be breathing a sigh of relief, especially the lower classes. Even the teachers were in a better mood than usual.

It had seemed as if Wednesday would never arrive, and Tommy had been waiting for this day ever since the weekend. At lunchtime, the football team results would be posted up on Main House notice board, and Tommy was confident his name would be on the list. The trials on Monday had gone better than he could have hoped: he had scored three goals and saved another two while in goal. Simon and the others had congratulated him afterwards, and to top it all, yesterday Simon had stopped Tommy in the hallway after biology,

'The lads and I were wondering if you'd like to join our gang.'

Tommy could not believe his ears.

'Yeah, that would be great,' he replied, beaming from ear to ear.

'That's settled then. We'll let you know when we next meet up and, Tommy, welcome to The Pioneers.'

And there was another reason Tommy could not wait for Wednesday to arrive. A reason that was even more important than football. Last night, after finishing the washing up and making a pot of tea for his parents, Tommy had plucked up the courage to ask the question that had been burning inside him all evening.

'Mum, can I cycle to school tomorrow?'

'Well, I don't know—'

'It would save you taking me.'

'But I'm not sure about—'

'You could have a lie in. I'll get breakfast ready.'

'Oh, now there's an idea. What do you think, Gordon?' Her husband grunted a couple of times. 'Well, okay, but remember Sally only eats her special bread with her organic strawberry jam.'

Cycling to school meant Tommy would be able to see Mr Petrovsky on his way home. He was almost bursting with the story of Perseus and Pegasus.

It was not too difficult to keep his adventures a secret. Most people would think he was either completely mad or telling lies if he confided in them, but to have no one to share them with was proving hard. He felt different: more grownup and able to take care of himself. He felt a quiet confidence inside him. A confidence that had given him the strength to stand up to the Twins. And to his mum.

*

It was now ten past twelve, and Tommy was standing by the noticeboard in Main Hall. A large crowd had formed around it in the last few minutes as the boys spilled out of their morning classes and rushed over to await the football results.

'Hey, Tommy.' He was poked in the ribs by one of his classmates, Nigel, who always hung around with Simon. Tommy had never spoken to him before.

'I've got a note for you from Simon,' said Nigel secretly, slipping a crumpled piece of paper into Tommy's hand. 'Should have given it to you at break time, but I forgot.' He hung his head and looked rather miserable. 'Sorry. Please don't tell Simon. It's the first time he's asked me to do something, and I've already made a mess.'

'Don't worry. I'll read it now,' Tommy whispered. His fingers itched to open it.

'Thing is, it's in code,' said Nigel despondently.

'Cripes, any idea what code?'

'Don't know,' said Nigel even more wretchedly. 'Hope you'll be able to break it in time.' With a downhearted sigh, Nigel slipped away into the crowd and vanished from sight.

Before he could unfold the note, Tommy saw Mr Adams, the sports master, come strolling up to the noticeboard. He was clutching the football results. Everyone around him darted forward as he pinned them up. Tommy slipped the note into his pocket and rushed forward to join the crowd.

The din grew louder as the boys in front called out names from the lists. Tommy pushed his way to the front and scanned the neatly typed pieces of paper. Year Ten, Year Eight. Then he saw it. Top of the list:

Tommy Turner (Captain)   Centre Forward

He had done it! Captain! He stared at his name. Awesome! Just wait until he told Digby. His parents might even be proud of him for a change.

Other people were calling it out to their friends.

'Turner. Tommy Turner is captain.'

'You know. The one who stood up to the Higgins Twins.'

'He's got a wicked kick.'

'Good one, Tommy. Congratulations.' Simon yanked him out of the crowd. 'Did you see? I'm in as goalie.'

'Hey that's great,' said Tommy, bursting with excitement. 'We're going to win the school cup this year, just you wait and see.'

'You bet. We're going to slaughter the others 'til they won't know what's hit them.'

'Reduce them to pulp.' Tommy grinned, imagining the Cup in his hands.

'You bet.' Simon leant in towards Tommy and whispered, 'You got the note?'

Tommy nodded, but before he could say anything about the code, Simon continued in a hushed voice, 'Great. I'll see you there in ten minutes, then,' and he dashed off towards the stairs.

Tommy touched his pocket. The corners of the note felt hard beneath the fabric. What did it say? He had to get away from the crowd so he could read it, try to decipher what it meant. He hurried through Main Hall, which was filling up with ravenous lunchers. Sounds of scraping chairs and discarded cutlery echoed around the old panelled room. Boys meandered to and fro with food-laden trays, seeking out their friends. Tommy's stomach rumbled at the smell of macaroni cheese, but there was no time for lunch. He had to meet Simon in ten minutes, but where he had no idea.

At the end of the hall lay the library, out of bounds except at specific times of the day when it was run like a military operation by one of the teachers. Tommy glanced around. No one was watching. He reached out and turned the doorknob. The door slid open with a gentle click, and Tommy slipped inside.

The room was cool and silent. Bookcases lined every wall as far as the eye could see. Normally, the room would lure its guests into a quiet reverie, but today Tommy had no time to lose. He hurried over to one of the chairs, took out the note and unfolded it. The page was full of squares and dots.

Tommy stared blindly at the paper, willing the symbols to change into words. Squares and Vs and dots inside some of them—what could it mean? He had no idea how to start. *This is ridiculous*, he thought angrily. *I'll never be able to break the code in time.*

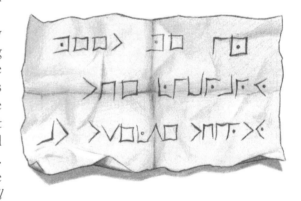

He glanced at his watch, two minutes to go. *I'll kill Nigel next time I see him*, he vowed, imagining the rest of his friendless days at High Brooms. Why would anyone possibly want to be friends with Useless Tommy? No gangs, no fun, nothing. All because of Nigel and the stupid code.

Tommy scanned the room in despair. *Wait, that's it—the library computer!* He rushed over to the desk. It was on, thank goodness, and warm. Someone must have only just left the library. Quickly he typed *code squares dots* into the search engine. Up came images of QR codes. *Aghhh,* Tommy slammed his fist on the desk in frustration. One minute left. Scrolling down—*There—there.* The Pigpen Cipher. *Thank you, Wiki,* he thought as he clicked the link.

Up came images of Tic Tac Toe grids with letters in them. *Of course, that's it; each shape's a letter.* He placed the note on the desk, glancing from screen to paper. *Two squares together—Es, those are Es— the shape before with the dot—where is it, where is it—there! An M—*

Quickly Tommy worked through the letters: *MEET ME IN THE L—*

A sudden noise broke into his work. Footsteps. Someone was coming into the room. Tommy exited the search engine, grabbed the note from the desk and, scouring around for a good hiding place, ducked behind one of the long velvet curtains. The footsteps stopped. Tommy drew himself deeper inside the curtains and held his breath as a grating sound took their place. He peeked round the curtain. It was coming from one of the bookshelves. One of the bookcases was slowly moving forward.

The gap yawned its way open until a dark void was visible within. And then a head appeared around the corner.

Tommy Turner's Tremendous Travels

✋ Chapter 17 ✍

The Pioneers

'Simon!' Tommy whispered his name as loud as he dared, and Simon hurried over to him.

'You broke the code then,' Simon said, looking impressed. 'Took me ages to work anything out when I first learnt it.'

Tommy, shrugging as innocently as possible, changed the subject.

'A secret passage? Where does it go to?'

'Come on, I'll show you,' said Simon, leading the way back. 'Scott discovered it last week when he had to clean out the bathrooms as a punishment the prefects gave him. Had to scrub the showers for a whole week. But it was better than facing Mr Hargreeves.' Simon flicked on his torch as the bookcase swung closed behind them. 'Anyway, he found the opening behind the back wall of the cleaning cupboard. It was all boarded up and cobwebby, but we managed to prise it open without too much effort.

'We're going to the bathrooms, are we?' asked Tommy, trying not to show his disappointment. A secret passage should lead somewhere better than a bathroom.

'No, not today. The passage also leads down to the cellars, and that's where we're meeting. Come on, the others are waiting.'

Simon led the way along the tight, musty passage, Tommy following as silently as possible. Through the walls he could hear the muffled noise of lunchtime in Main Hall. *We must be going past the teachers' table right now*, thought Tommy, smiling at their secret. They crept on in silence, past Main Hall, past the kitchens, around one corner, then another, until finally two sets of steps came into view, one which Simon said led up to the dormitories, the other down towards the cellar. Simon turned right and descended.

The passage opened out into a dusty stone room. Its walls were lined with broken shelves, most of which looked as though they were hanging on for dear life by a single screw. Cobwebs the size of football nets dangled from the ceiling, the spiders having long since claimed the room as their own.

In the centre sat the gang, each one silhouetted by the beam of his own torch. They were sharing out the heap of goodies piled in the middle.

'Hope you've left some grub for us,' said Simon, he and Tommy rushing over to join them. 'I'm starving.' He turned to Tommy to explain. 'We raided our tuck boxes last night. Poor Nigel got caught by Matron and pretended he had stomach ache. She made him take a huge spoonful of milk of magnesia, didn't she, Nige?'

'Yrruck,' exclaimed Nigel, pulling a sickly face. 'That stuff makes you sicker than before.'

'That'll teach you not to get caught again. Have a Mars Bar, Tommy and let me introduce everyone.'

There were four other boys in the gang besides Tommy and Simon. Nigel, who stammered his apologies again for forgetting the note, was rather small and rotund, a result of the enormous food parcels his mum sent every week.

'He's got goop for brains, ain't ya, Nige,' joked Simon, elbowing him in the ribs.

'Yeh, but at least I've got Neil.' Nigel turned to Tommy. 'He's my brother, he's in Year Ten, he knows e-v'rything.'

Then there was Scott, who was as tall and lanky as Tommy, with a mischievous sparkle in his eyes.

'Congrats on being made captain. Thought you were awesome on the field,' he said, adding with pride, 'I'm playing defence.'

The next boy, Sebastian, was already familiar to Tommy as 'Brains'. He excelled at everything mathematical or scientific and seemed to know as much, if not more, than the teachers.

'And finally, this is my cousin, Will,' said Simon. 'He and I have been at High Brooms since Pre-Prep, and our dads were also here about a hundred years ago—isn't that right, Will?'

'Yes, if you look at the school photo of 1988, you can see my dad twice in the back row. He started on the left side and ran round the back to get in the picture again. Mr Hargreeves went ballistic when he found out and threatened to expel him.'

'So, Mr Hargreeves was headmaster back then?' asked Tommy.

'Deputy head, but still as vicious by all accounts. First thing he said when he met me was, "Hope you're not your father's son." Still, Dad's done alright.'

'Okay, okay, enough of that,' snapped Simon.

'Keep your shirt on, Si! Just 'cause your dad was the class swot.'

129

'Okay, lads, that's enough,' sighed Scott. 'We don't have time for your family feuds when there's lots to sort out for the mission.'

'What mission?' enquired Tommy, biting into his second Mars Bar.

'OTO, or rather Operation Twin Obliteration,' said Brains in his usual brisk way of talking.

'Yeah, we're going to annihilate them,' cried Scott, jumping up and practising a few karate kicks.

'What, you want to kill the Twins?' gulped Tommy.

'No stupid. We're just going to show them who's boss around here,' replied Simon, stuffing a handful of crisps into his mouth. 'Thebe hab id comn or alonb timb.'

'What?' chorused the others.

'He said, "They've had it coming for a long time",' replied Will.

Simon swallowed his mouthful. 'You bet. They've given us hell for the past two years, and it's about time they paid for it.'

The other boys chorused their agreement.

'Anyone know what's happening with the Twins?' asked Simon.

'From what Neil told me, they're coming out of sickbay this afternoon,' piped up Nigel. 'Stu's got his arm in a sling, but there's nothing wrong with Shaun.'

'That figures,' said Brains.

'How come he gets away with two days off school, when all Matron ever gives me is two Panadol and a lecture on reading after lights out?' huffed Scott, finishing off one of Nigel's mum's homemade muffins.

'That's because you're the lousiest actor I've ever seen,' retorted Will, giving Scott a playful slap.

'Anything more, Nige?' asked Tommy, anxious to get on with the planning.

'Well, yes, there is in fact,' gulped Nigel, turning a bright shade of cerise. 'It's just, I've forgotten what.'

'Oh Nigel, you great clod,' groaned Scott.

'Come on, think, will you?'

'Yeah, use that bit of gunk you call a brain.'

Nigel's brain was whirring so fast the boys could almost hear it. Then he leapt up and shouted, 'GOT IT!'

'WHAT!'

Plonking himself back on the floor, Nigel leant forward into the group. 'Neil also said this Friday they were implementing Plan A.'

'Plan A?' said Brains.

'What's Plan A?' shouted Scott, jumping around in frustration.

'Sit down, Scott,' said Simon, irritated now.

Tommy turned to Nigel. 'Any clue what Plan A is?'

'Well, as a matter of fact I have,' said Nigel indignantly. 'Last week, the Twins received a package. It caused rather a lot of attention 'cause it had come from China, but they assured Peterson, who was on prefect duty at the time, that it was herbal medicine their mum had ordered. Not sure what exactly was in it, but certainly nothing herbal, and Neil said they walked around with grins on their faces for the rest of the day. Anyway, rumour is they are planning to use whatever it is during school assembly on Friday. Maybe let off a stink bomb or something. I don't know all the details, but what I do know is they will try and pin it on someone else.'

'Tommy,' said Brains quietly.

The boys turned to stare at Tommy.

'After what you did to them on Monday, they'll do anything to get back at you,' said Simon.

'They've already declared *krieg* on you,' warned Will.

'*Krieg*?' said Tommy tightly.

'WAR,' replied Scott and Will together.

Tommy gulped, 'I may as well say goodbye to my teeth now.'

'Not if we can stop them before they get to you,' said Simon, trying to muster up some encouragement.

'Yeah, elimination's the only answer. Blast them to smithereens,' cried Scott, rattling off some imaginary rounds of ammunition.

'I think we should find out exactly what their plan is and try and stop it before it's too late,' suggested Will.

The other boys agreed this was the way to go and started suggesting ways to go about it, but Tommy sat there silently, thinking. *If we stop them now, they'll only find another way to get me, and I'm sure next time will be even worse.* No, it would be wrong to stop them from carrying out their nasty little plan.

'Listen, guys,' he started. 'I think it would be better to let them continue with their plan but make sure they're caught. That they get hauled up in front of Mr Hargreeves, not me.'

'Yeah, give them both suspension.'

'Expulsion?'

'Whatever. At least it will get them out of our lives and give them what they deserve.'

'Sounds good,' agreed Scott. 'Now, I suggest we keep our ears to the ground tonight, find out all we can and report back here tomorrow lunchtime to make plans.'

Chapter 18

Nicolas Petrovsky

Tommy watched the last sliver of butter disappear into the hot teacake; then he took a huge, yummy bite, feeling the gooey mess melting in his mouth and trickling down his fingers. He looked up at Mr Petrovsky, and the old man smiled.

'Taste good?'

Tommy nodded, his mouth too full of jam and butter.

The clock on the mantelpiece softly ticked away the minutes as a heavy silence lay in the room. Mr Petrovsky sat staring into the distance, trying to absorb Tommy's story.

'Perseus and Pegasus, Medusa and her sisters. It's just so fantastical,' he mused.

'Don't forget the baby giant,' said Tommy, licking his fingers.

'Oh yes, the baby giant. It's just so—incredible.'

'So was Yorintown,' said Tommy. 'It's funny, but I didn't feel scared about going back inside the cave or about facing the Gorgons. I kept thinking about what you had told me. That each adventure would be a new lesson for me.'

'Well, Tommy, you certainly showed your courage during this adventure and, may I say, great strength.'

'I suppose I did, but at the time it just felt natural, as if I were still linked to this world by an invisible thread. Once I got used to the fact that I definitely wasn't dreaming, that is.'

Tommy paused, uncertain how to phrase his next question. It seemed ridiculous to him, now he thought about it. All his strength and courage that had come so naturally only a few days ago had suddenly disappeared?

'Mr Petrovsky—'

The old man smiled at Tommy's fretful face. 'You've every right to feel fearful about another adventure. I would be, too, if I'd gone through what you had. You might have died, Tommy, if you hadn't had the flask from Yorintown. But you didn't. And you said yourself that you felt safe. Protected. Connected to your real life.'

'So, you think it's okay to go back again?'

'Wherever *back* may be,' laughed Mr Petrovsky. 'I think you will know when it's right to go and when it's not. You can choose. No one else. And just think of all the adventures you could be missing.'

'Then I'll do it. Tonight. I'll try again tonight,' said Tommy, his eyes widening at the thought.

Mr Petrovsky pushed the plate of teacakes towards Tommy. 'Go on, have the last one. You'll need your strength if this new adventure is anything like the others.'

Tommy grabbed the teacake and sat back in his chair, munching.

How he loved being in this room. This dusty, old room with its piles of papers and stacks of books. Here and his uncle's study were the two places where he felt most at home, as if he were as much a part of the furniture as the dilapidated old sofas and tatty lampshades. And then there was Mr Petrovsky, who knew just the right thing to say and do.

Tommy finished off the teacake and licked the jam off the corners of his mouth.

'Mr Petrovsky,' he started, 'will you tell me about yourself now? Who you are and where you come from?'

Mr Petrovsky nodded. 'I promised you, didn't I—my goodness, where should I start?' He poured the last dregs of tea into his cup and stirred it, deep in thought. Tommy wriggled himself into a more comfortable position and waited. Finally, the old man started his tale.

'The world of my childhood is almost unimaginable to you or even, I would think, to your parents, and yet it was only sixty-six years ago when my father and I left Russia. Those sixty-odd years have seen so many changes to mankind. Space travel. Computers. The Internet. Mobile phones. Who, in those days, would have thought these things possible? Not me. Was it even important to us? No. We had barely enough food to eat, clothes to wear or medicine to keep the old or weak from dying. In winter, it was so cold we would wear our boots and coats in the house and huddle around the fire just to keep warm.'

Mr Petrovsky shivered at his ghosts of the past.

'Don't think I'm complaining. It's just there seems to be so much greed in the world today. So much is taken for granted. A new car, a bigger house, holidays, food on the table. Everything is available, bought and thrown away with the same amount of ease.'

'But why didn't you have enough food?' asked Tommy, feeling rather ashamed of the three teacakes he had just consumed without thought.

'Well, the 1930s and 40s were a terrible time for many people in Russia, especially those opposed to the regime. My family lived in a remote farming community at the foothills of the Ural Mountains. It was a breathtakingly beautiful place: rugged mountains, crystal clear waters. But it was also terribly harsh, particularly in wintertime when the snow would lie on the ground for months at a time.

'The farmers in our district were called *kulaks*. We didn't agree with what the government was doing to our communities, stealing our grain and taking our animals, and because of this, the MGB—Stalin's Secret Army—were constantly threatening us. They forced many families to leave their homes. Many of my friends and their families were taken and never heard of again.'

'Who did you live with?' asked Tommy, trying to imagine what it must have been like to grow up in such hardship.

'My parents and grandmother. I did have an older brother, but he died while I was a baby from a disease called haemophilia.'

'What's hemefila?' asked Tommy, attempting to pronounce the word.

Mr Petrovsky corrected him kindly, 'Haemophilia. It means you're born with blood that doesn't clot. So, if you get cut or whatever, you can't heal properly. My mother used to call me her miracle baby because I was born disease free.'

'And were your parents very poor?'

'Not as poor as some. We lived in an old wooden cottage on the outskirts of the village that had been home to my grandmother since she was a child. Imagine that, Tommy, living in one place for your whole life.'

'It sounds pretty boring,' said Tommy with honesty, his mind flitting back to the summer when he had been desperate not to move home. *All these adventures I would have missed, the friends I would never have known.*

'Well, we didn't have time to be bored,' Mr Petrovsky continued. 'Our lives depended on working hard. My father would be out no matter the weather, ploughing fields or sowing seeds. We didn't have tractors or machinery to help us, as they had been confiscated, and most of our farm animals had been slaughtered, so he pulled the plough himself. It was exhausting, physical work, but at least it gave us enough food for the table, unlike many thousands of people. You know, Tommy, some people were so hungry that they ate grass and tree bark just to survive. Can you imagine that?

'In the evenings, we would all sit round the fire in the kitchen. Sometimes my mother would sing in her soft, velvet voice. Songs of different times and strange languages.' Mr Petrovsky paused, mesmerised by the distant memory.

'My father would smile at her and call her *vasha vysota*, your highness. I always knew how much they adored and depended on each other. He would make her tiny wooden dolls, just to bring a smile to her face. He was so meticulous in his work, carving each detail to perfection. That is how we ended up running Petrovsky's Toy Store. When we first came to England, my father made dolls and puppets for a living. We could not believe the price people would pay for them. He was so successful that, within a few years, we could afford to open this shop.'

'And your grandmother? What was she like?'

'My *babushka*? She was the heart of the family. She worked just as hard as my father, especially when the harvest had to be brought in. Mother did, too, but there was always something different about her. I didn't realise it as a child. Then, she was simply my mother, but as I grew up my memories of her became clearer. She had an elegance and grace about her that was unlike anyone else I have ever known, but also a great sadness. As though sometime in her life she had witnessed a terrible tragedy. We never talked about it, and I was too young to understand, but I do remember I would sometimes find her sitting, staring into the unknown as though she was captured by another world.'

'Why didn't she come to England with you?'

Mr Petrovsky looked at Tommy, his watery eyes tinged with anguish, but deep inside them a steel anger still burned. The words he spoke next were choked with emotion.

'My mother was killed. Murdered by those hateful Stalinists. Murdered and then burned almost beyond recognition. We didn't even have time to bury her. We didn't even say goodbye. My father and I just ran for our lives.'

A tear fell down his cheek. Mr Petrovsky brushed it away. Silent minutes ticked by again and again. Tommy could feel the old man's grief washing over him; what he should do, what should he say? What *could* he do? What *could* he say? Finally, the clock struck six.

The old man looked up, his face wracked with anxious lines, as though he was bursting with some awful secret. But all he said was, 'You'd better be off home, don't you think?'

But Tommy did not want to leave his friend alone. Not at a time like this.

'It's fine, go home. I'll be fine.'

'Are you sure?' Tommy asked.

'Yes, yes, I'm sure.' Suddenly, he grabbed Tommy's arm. 'Tommy, promise me you'll come back on Friday. You have to come on Friday. Can you do this?'

'Yes, of course. Of course, I'll come after school,' said Tommy, surprised by the urgency in Mr Petrovsky's voice.

The old man sank back in his chair, his hands clasping his head, muttering to himself, '*Blagodarite, chto bog*, thank you God. Thank you, Tommy, thank you. Please go now, leave me—leave me to my thoughts.'

*

What a day this has been, Tommy thought as he cycled home. So many things had happened it was hard to know what to chew over first. The Pioneers! That was great—he was in the coolest gang of his year, and they wanted to help him sort out the Higgins Twins— Tommy gulped—*the Higgins Twins!* Now that was not so great. He really did not want to meet the end of Shaun's fist, or Stu's for that matter. But at least the gang had a plan, and they had until Friday to sort everything out.

Friday! Mr Petrovsky! What was that all about? His friend had looked so miserable, and Tommy had felt so helpless. But he had promised he would be there on Friday, and he would be there, come what may—even if it meant his mum grounding him for three weeks afterwards.

He gulped again—his mum! Okay, so she had let him cycle to school today, and that was a big step forward, but he wished she could just be a normal mum. That he did not have to try so hard. That she would be proud of him as well as Sally. And she should be, of course she should. He was, after all, football captain.

Football captain! Captain of the football team.

Oh yes, what a day this has been!

And it was not even over yet. Tonight was another adventure. Tonight, Tommy would wear his T-shirt.

Tommy Turner's Tremendous Travels

⤾ Chapter 19 ⤿

The World Cup Finals

'OWUUUCH!'

Someone, or something, had kicked Tommy fair and square in his bottom and sent him flying through the air. He flung out his arms and legs to stop the fall but—

Where were his arms? Where were his legs? They appeared to be stuck tight to his body, motionless, useless, and the ground was rapidly approaching.

A whistle blew, and someone shouted, 'FOUL!'

And then *THUD*, he landed on the football pitch, rolling over and over until he felt dizzy with pain. The players were running towards him. He tried to get up but only managed to roll some more. They were nearly on top of him.

'Watch it!' he yelled, but it was no use. No one could hear him amongst the chants of the crowd.

'England! England! Come on, you Lions!'

A hand reached down to grab him. *It's—no—it can't be. But—yes, it is. Eddie Bates.*

Eddie Bates, the best player in England, was going to help him to his feet.

Tommy grinned, *Maybe I can get his autograph later*, he thought, but then the strangest thing happened. Eddie Bates picked him right off the ground and threw him straight towards another player.

And then it dawned on him.

What the—I'm not playing in this match.

I'm not a player at all.

I am the FOOTBALL.

HELP!

The crowd was going wild, screaming, throwing their hands in the air, chanting, 'Kemp. Kemp. Give us your best shot!'

Tommy tried to yell, 'No, don't shoot. Get another ball,' but it was useless. All that came out was the tiniest bit of air.

He was positioned carefully on the muddy ground.

In the distance, the wall of opposition players was lining up, beyond, the white net of the goal. It looked so tiny from this angle. Straining around, he watched Daryl Kemp shake his ankles and then come speeding towards him.

Tommy flinched inside and—*WHACK*—he was rocketed up into the air by Kemp's golden foot.

AAAAUUUGGGHH!

Tommy hurtled through the air, players leaping at all angles, trying to head him. *Out of the way*, he thought, pulling himself into a tight knot and whizzing past. He could see the mouth of the goal speeding towards him, the goalie crouching low, menacing, ready to pounce at any second.

Higher, higher, he thought. *Come on, you can do it.*

The goalie leapt up, soaring into the air, his arm growing longer and longer. Tommy was heading right for his glove.

NOOOOOOWWWWW!

THWACK!

He flew straight into the back of the net, brushing the goalie's fingertips, and landed inside the magical white line.

'GOAL TO ENGLAND!'

The crowd went ballistic, their flags and banners waving madly, screaming, chanting, 'KEMP! KEMP!'

The goalie picked himself up from the back of the net, swearing and muttering to himself, '*Mon Dieu, deux deux et moins d'une minute de jeu!*'

What was that? French? We're playing France.

But what had he said?

Tommy was picked up and before he had time to catch his breath, booted straight into the middle of the field by the Frenchman's angry kick.

Two all and less than one minute to play.

He felt like a bird, whizzing through the air, feeling the wind catch his face. *It's quite nice up here*, he thought, *quieter away from the crowds and certainly not so painful. Maybe I'll stay up a bit longer.*

He looked down at the field below. The players had stopped running and were gawping at him; some were scratching their heads and pointing in amazement. The ball looked as though it was stuck in the air. Not just stuck but getting higher and higher.

('Well folks, what a phenomenal kick.'

'Yes, Gary. I have to say that in all my years of commentating, I've never seen such a kick.')

Tommy saw a bird flying towards him. *Hello there*, he thought. The bird squawked in terror and flew off.

He looked down at the pitch, seeing the ant-like players scurrying about underneath him. Just as he felt he could go no higher, his stomach lurched into his feet and he plummeted to the ground.

Down, down, down, like a rocket. Turning and twisting in an endless dive to the ground. Players running towards him, blue shirts

143

mingled with white, every eye focused on his fall. He rushed towards them, the ground enlarging at every millisecond. He could make out their faces now, right underneath him: Gagnon, Leroy, Fairbairn.

If I can make it to Fairbairn, he thought, inching his body to the right.

But one second before contact, Gagnon spun forward and— *BAM*—Tommy was booted towards the England goal.

No, no this can't be happening. The goal was zooming ever nearer, Wayne Wiggins crouching at the front.

I have to stop, he thought. *BRAKE.*

('Incredible, Gary. The ball's slowed right down.'

'Yes, he must have put too much spin on it.')

The French fans groaned. The English fans cheered. Wayne Wiggins caught him. Twenty seconds to go. *WHACK!* He was booted back into the centre of the field. There was Hendridge. *On his head, on his head.*

BIFF! Soaring up again. Drake right underneath. Tumbling down and—Drake's magical feet dribbling like an express train.

OOH, OOH, OUCH, OOH, AGH, OOH, OUCH.

THWACK! Spinning around. *Where is the goal?* Eddie Bates rushing up, foot poised.

BAM! Soaring ahead, blue shirts running, whizzing past. *Curve a bit, curve a bit.*

SMASH!!! Into the net. Screaming, cheering, whistling, yelling. *I've done it, I've done it.* The referee's whistle blowing. Game over.

ENGLAND VICTORIOUS!

Tommy lay at the back of the net, bruised but buoyant, exhausted and exhilarated. All around, players were stripping off, swapping shirts, running around the pitch and waving at their loyal fans. The atmosphere was electric.

England had won the World Cup.

Cheers rose up again and again, swelling the noise to deafening levels. The commentators were going mad.

('Truly unbelievable, how the ball swerved just at the last second.'

'Yes, Gary. Almost as if it had a life of its own.'

'Well, we've done it, folks. The cup is finally coming back to England.')

*

The first thing Tommy did when he woke up was pull a large clump of grass out of his mouth. Yuck. He was covered with mud and bruises, soaking wet and slimy. His bedclothes looked as though a cow had slept in them.

But what an amazing night that had been. If only he could play like that always—as a player not the ball, obviously—then they would win the school cup for sure and perhaps even the county championships.

He stared up at the ceiling, remembering how cool it had been to soar through the air like—well, like a World Cup football. What was that all about? Did he really have the possibility to become anything, anywhere? Did he really want to? Yes, if it meant England being world champions but he would not really like to be stuck for the rest of his life as a milk bottle or something. *Although,* Tommy chuckled to himself, *imagine what a mess I could make when Sally tried to pour some milk.*

He hauled himself off the bed—it was time to get ready for school—and looked again at the crumpled, grass-stained mess he had left behind. How would he explain that to his mum? He could hear her shrieking up the stairs, giving him five to 'Get down here.' Then his dad yelling from the bedroom: telling him to 'Get a move on.'

But it did not matter. None of it mattered. Because he, Tommy Turner, had won the World Cup. He had been kicked by Kemp, dribbled by Drake, headed by Hendridge, and booted through the air by his all-time hero, Eddie Bates. What could be better than that?

❧ Chapter 20 ❧

School Assembly

Friday morning. Tommy woke with a start and a tummy full of nerves—The Higgins Twins. Today was either going to end in triumph or a set of broken teeth. He thought back to yesterday when the gang had met during lunch. Nigel had arrived with a chilling message, 'Neil saw me at break-time—apparently Stu and Shaun left sickbay this morning.' The colour drained from his face, and he turned to Tommy. 'You know that *krieg* they declared on you—well, apparently it's nuclear.'

Tommy pulled the bedclothes up over his head; perhaps he could pull a sickie and just stay at home. He coughed a couple of times and practised speaking in a husky whisper, but he knew his mum would chuck him out of the house anyway. No, it was time to get up and face his demons. Stumbling out of bed in a jittery unease, Tommy pulled on his uniform and headed downstairs.

Sally was sitting in the kitchen, eating her organic bread and jam. Tommy grabbed himself a bowl of cereal and stood munching it by the sink. He heard his dad calling out goodbye, then watched through the window as he clambered into the car and drove off at his usual high speed.

Sally gave a sudden cry, and before Tommy had a chance to turn around, he heard the thud on the floor. A seizure. He grabbed a handful of tea towels from the drawer and rushed to Sally's aid. His sister was lying rigid on her side, her mouth in a tight grimace. He pushed aside her chair and stuffed the towels under her head.

'Mum—Mum,' he yelled, 'quick—it's Sally.' He turned back just as Sally started jerking and shuddering. Inside, Tommy's heart was pumping like a piston, but he had gone through the routine before and his head remained clear.

'Mum—Mum,' Tommy called again. Sally's whole body was shaking by now, but there was nothing Tommy could do except soothe and protect her until the seizure stopped. He looked at Sally's glazed stare, remembering how frightened he had been the first time this had happened. Where was Mum? Upstairs 'doing her face' no doubt.

At last, Sally began to quieten, and Tommy was placing her in the recovery position when his mum entered the kitchen.

'You wanted me?' she snapped, stopping in her tracks as she took in the scene. 'Oh, my darling, let Mummy come and help you,' she cried, rushing over to Sally and smothering her in red lipstick kisses, threatening to undo the good Tommy had done.

'Let her be, Mum. She needs to rest,' he said, exasperated by her actions. But his mum was too busy fussing over his sister to notice. Tommy stood watching for a moment, confused by the wave of protectiveness he felt for his sister. Then it dawned on him—this was his moment to escape. 'Don't worry, Mum, I'll cycle in today.' Tommy grabbed his schoolbag and headed for the door. 'I'll be home about six,' he cried, banging the door shut behind him before his mum had a chance to reply.

*

Main Hall was bursting with pupils by the time Tommy pulled up on his bike. Some of the older boys were milling around outside, no doubt planning how to escape assembly time and hoping they could sneak into the bushes for a forbidden smoke. But today Tommy had no time to lose. Quick as a flash, he jumped off his bike and rushed inside to meet the gang.

He found Simon and Brains huddled together in the corner next to the noticeboard, as they had prearranged yesterday lunchtime. They were going through the plans and looking far more suspicious than they should. Simon turned to Tommy as soon as he saw him.

'There you are. Where've you been?' he asked crossly.

'Sorry, I had a bit of trouble at home, but it's sorted out now.'

'Come on then,' huffed Simon, heading towards the main body of the hall, 'Mr Hargreeves will be here any minute.' Breakfast had ended fifteen minutes earlier than usual that morning and, while the stragglers were wolfing down the last of their cornflakes, the hall had been transformed for School Assembly. Row upon row of chairs were spread throughout the entire hall. The noise was deafening, groups of excited boys yelling to their friends and laughing raucously at dirty jokes. Simon led them to the seats that Nigel was frantically trying to save at the end of one of the far rows.

'About time. Nearly got into a fight when Stepshaw tried to bag the seats.'

'Sorry, my fault,' said Tommy.

'Just sit down and do try to act normally, will you?' Simon said to Nigel, who was bouncing up and down in anticipation.

'Normal?' joked Brains. 'Nigel?'

'Ha-ha,' said Simon, not amused. 'Now does everyone remember what to do?'

'Yes,' they chorused.

'Keep your voices down, ears everywhere,' whispered Simon. 'Now, Will and Scott are in position upstairs on the balcony. Just keep your eyes open. We don't know where the Twins will strike from. All we can do for now is sit tight and wait.'

They did not have to wait at all, for at that moment Mr Hargreeves appeared at the main entrance with the rest of the teachers. The din in the hall ground to a halt as the procession made their way through the throng of pupils towards the high table at the front of the hall, Mr Hargreeves glaring ferociously at the crowd as he marched up the gangway. The high table was set on a large podium, which meant the teachers could get a good view of any misbehaviour. Behind it, the enormous main stairs, out of bounds to all except teachers and prefects, swept its way up to the Main House dorms and along the balcony towards the Headmaster's offices.

Mr Hargreeves remained standing while the other teachers took their seats. Once the chair scraping had diminished, he raised his hand.

'Teachers, prefects, pupils,' he began, his lofty voice ringing through the hall. 'Today is a historic day for High Brooms. A historic day, indeed, for it was one hundred and fifty years ago on this very day that Edmond Hasslebank opened these very doors to the first pupils of our renowned and—Stevens, my office straight after Assembly,' he bellowed at an older boy, who had been mimicking his haughty speech, '—our renowned and remarkable school. Before I say a few words to commemorate our wonderful founder, let us first sing *Jerusalem*. Mr Andrews, if you please.'

Mr Andrews struck the first few chords of *Jerusalem* on the piano, and the whole school rose and sang.

> And did those feet in ancient time
> Walk upon England's mountain green?

Is that a shadow darting along the balcony, thought Tommy, *or am I dreaming?*

There it was again. A dark figure, bent double, hurrying towards the staircase. He nudged Simon's elbow, beckoning toward the front of the hall.

> And was the holy Lamb of God
> On England's pleasant pastures seen?

The figure disappeared from view at the top of the stairs, high above the assembled crowd.

> And was Jerusalem builded here
> Amongst those dark satanic mills?

Just as the first verse ended, Tommy noticed a hand appearing over the side of the closed banisters.

> Bring me my bow of burning gold!

There. Right above Mr Hargreeves' head.

> Bring me my arrows of desire!

The hand was holding a small pepper pot. The hand was now shaking the pepper pot vigorously, and out was tumbling a large cloud of fine white powder.

> I will not cease from mental fight
> Nor shall my sword sleep in my hand,

The powder was now wafting gently downwards, dispersing throughout the hall.

> Till we have built Jerusalem
> In England's green and pleasant—

'AWWWWCHOO!'

Mr Hargreeves let out the most enormous sneeze, which exploded onto the prefects sitting on the front row. 'My apologies,' he barked, blowing his nose on the large handkerchief he withdrew from his breast pocket. The prefects looked none too amused as they wiped themselves clean.

Mr Hargreeves cleared his throat. 'Edmond Hasslebank was a most distinguished and—Aaa-AAA-awwwwchoooo!'

His sneeze resounded throughout the hall, rattling some of the ancient windowpanes.

'—distinguished and—AWWWCHOOO!'

Something resembling a Yorkshire terrier flew across the table. Mr Hargreeves, howling in outrage, clutched his now shiny and very bald head. His wig rocketed through the air and, after making a final pirouette as delicately as a prima ballerina, landed squarely on the Head Boy's lap in front of the whole assembled school.

'AWWCHOOO,' sneezed Mr Philips.

'AAA…AAACHOOO,' sneezed Mr Davies.

'AAAWWWCHOOO,' sneezed Mr Hargreeves.

Soon the whole high table and first four rows of prefects and pupils were doubled over, sneezing vigorously. Mr Hargreeves was scrabbling for his wig—which the Head Boy had accidentally used as a handkerchief—and looked as if he might involuntarily combust at any moment.

'Quick, cover your noses before we start, too,' cried Simon, leaping out of the row. 'Nigel, Brains, up the back stairs and try to head off the Twins. Tommy, we'll take the main ones; they've got to be stopped.'

The boys tore off amid the deafening sneezes that were now spreading throughout the hall. Pupils large and small, fat and thin were sneezing, laughing, crying, standing, falling, unable to control the effect of the powder.

Mr Hargreeves had managed to regain his wig, which was now perched on his head like a straggly mop head. 'Order. Order,' he hollered, banging his fist on the table to try to restore calm.

But the entire hall was in chaos. Chairs were upturned as pupils clutched their sides, unable to breathe from laughter. Teachers were turning various shades of red as they tried, but failed, to control their outbursts.

Tommy and Simon sped over to Main Stairs and, crouching low, mounted them two at a time. At the top of the stairs, they turned right, flew through to the dorm area, and then zoomed up another winding staircase that led to the Year Eleven dorms. As they neared the top of the stairs, they could hear yelling coming from the long corridor

BANG. Through the fire door they raced and straight into Stu, who was hanging upside down from one of the old beams, his foot caught firmly in a noose.

'Ouch, me arm. Lemme down,' he shrieked, spinning round and round as he struggled to get free.

Will and Scott were squirming about on a large wriggling duvet cover from which muffled yells were emerging.

'Geroff me. Lemme go,' it howled.

At that moment, Nigel and Brains sped through the door at the other end of the corridor and pulled up alongside the others.

'About time,' cried Scott, bouncing on the duvet cover to shut it up. 'Give us a hand; we can't hold on much longer.'

The duvet cover reared up, and Will and Scott fell into a pile on the floor. Nigel and Brains leapt onto the heap, with Tommy close behind, but it was too late. The duvet cover ripped open, and Shaun came tumbling out.

'Stu, help,' he yelled, launching himself at Tommy and flattening him in one swoop. The other boys dived on top, while Stu watched helplessly from his captivity.

'Geroff me,' cried Shaun again, flailing wildly with his arms. Tommy was stuck underneath him, panting for breath, his face squashed firmly between Shaun's bottom and the wooden floor.

'Get his arms,' shouted Simon.

'Legs,' bellowed Brains, and the boys scrambled around, trying to locate the right limbs.

Just then, the fire door swung open and in marched Matron on dorm check duty. She nearly fainted at the sight of Stu hanging upside down and a mountain of squirming boys rolling around in a pile.

'Stop this IMMEDIATELY!' she ordered, drawing herself up to her full height and peering at them over her enormous chest.

The gang jumped at the sound of her voice. No one had noticed her entrance, and it was too late now. They rolled off Shaun and scrambled to their feet. Shaun sat in a heap on the floor and started to cry. Tommy patted himself on the head to make sure it was still the right shape; thankfully, it was still in one piece.

'Get him down, this instant,' barked Matron, pointing at Stu. 'What on earth is going on? Who started this?'

'The Twins,' shouted Simon.

'Turner,' yelled Shaun, pointing an accusing finger.

'Get off the floor, Higgins. You ought to be ashamed of yourself. Do you have an explanation, Turner?' she sneered, turning to Tommy with a glare that said, 'Yuck, how I dislike nasty, smelly boys and, ha, how wonderful to find them up to no good.'

'We saw the Twins with the sneezing powder and followed them up here,' said Tommy hopefully.

'Liar,' cried Shaun. 'He started it. Me and Stu are innocent.'

'That's not true,' exclaimed Simon.

'And he helped him,' said Shaun, warming to the tale. 'Him and the others. We were on our way to tell you when they attacked us.'

Matron was shaking with thunderous anger.

'Right, all of you, Mr Hargreeves's office immediately. We'll let him get to the bottom of this. Quick march.'

Matron frogmarched them through the fire door, back down the stairs and along the corridors, the boys glancing nervously to each other at the thought of the fate awaiting them when Mr Hargreeves found out what they had been up to.

'What's going to happen to us, Simon?' whispered Tommy, managing to catch up with his friend.

'You don't want to know, you really don't. Will had to see Hargreeves last year, and he couldn't eat for three days afterwards.'

'Three days,' gulped Tommy. What if he was suspended? If his parents found out about this? He shuddered at the thought of their fury. He would have to leave home. Run away. Yes, it would be best if he just disappeared.

'And that fact Matron caught us,' continued Simon with a tremble, 'is just about the very worst thing possible. Nothing pleases her more than a possible expulsion, and today there could be eight in one go.'

❧ Chapter 21 ☙

Revenge of the Higgins Twins

Assembly was over, ruined by the sneezing powder attack. The hall looked like carnage, upended chairs strewn throughout the room, the top table lying overturned on its side. Chaos ruled throughout the school, the usual watertight discipline having vanished into thin air. Classes were cancelled for the morning, as the teachers were in no fit state to hold any lessons. Most of the boys were back in their dorms, or milling around outside, delighted to have some time off.

'Wait here and don't move an inch if you value your lives,' gloated Matron as she led the boys through to the antechambers of the headmaster's office. She scowled at them as she rapped loudly on Mr Hargreeves's door. From within, a muffled voice shouted, 'Enter,' and she disappeared through.

Tommy and the gang crowded together in a nervous row. The silent room echoed with past punishments, expulsions and the *thwack* of a birch cane.

The Higgins Twins stood glaring from the corner of the room.

'Just you wait, Turner,' threatened Shaun with a low growl.

The door swung open and Matron reappeared. 'Headmaster will see you now,' she snarled, a faint smirk lingering around her mouth. 'Oh, and he's vowed to expel whoever is responsible for this utter outrage.'

Slowly, silently, the boys filed into the room. In the centre stood the great desk, its leather surface worn to a shine by decades of headmasters' elbows. Above it, a grim portrait of Edmond

Hasslebank presided over the impending punishment as he had done for the past one hundred and fifty years.

Mr Hargreeves stood by the window, his back to the room, his rage unabated. The bitter taste of humiliation lay fresh in his mouth. Now was his time for revenge. He could feel his victims' fear seeping into his skin, stoking the strength he needed to extract a confession. This is how he always stood when he was about to punish a pupil. Make them wait, make them sweat, tremble with fear. It gave him power. Power he believed was his right. But still, sometimes in the middle of the night, he tossed and turned and remembered the bullying he had endured throughout his school years. Well, now he was headmaster all that had changed. He could instil the same fear in these hateful boys.

He turned to face his victims, willing the boys to laugh at his wig. He need not have worried, though. His wig was the last thing on any of their minds. They were all mesmerised by his bright red nose, which was throbbing like a beacon from all the sneezing. As he opened his mouth to speak, it sprang to life, wobbling up and down with each word he uttered.

'Close the door, Matron,' he said grimly, 'and tell me again what you just witnessed.'

'Well, Headmaster,' she simpered, rubbing her stubby fingers in glee. 'I am shocked, shocked at the wickedness of these unruly children, who have made a mockery of our sacred school. Who have scandalised the very heart of our establishment. Who have brought shame and despair to—'

'Yes, yes, this is all very true. But WHAT did you see?' said Mr Hargreeves briskly.

Matron bristled at the interruption, then smiled her saccharine smile.

'Ah well, I have by my own cunning discovered the perpetrators of this heinous crime. The instigators of disgraceful and immoral atrocities. The very disease that plagues our otherwise peaceful—'

'Yes, yes, YES!' Mr Hargreeves's nose bounced up and down with anger. 'I know all that, but who exactly is the ringleader?'

'Well, with my vast experience and knowledge of the criminal mind, he is.' Matron raised her arm and pointed directly at Tommy.

'No. That's not true.'

'It's them.'

'They did it.'

The room was awash with voices aghast at Matron's accusation.

Tommy stared horror-stuck. How could this be happening? It was all wrong. And his mum—what would she say? What if he got expelled? She would never forgive him. The Higgins Twins smiled with delight. They were going to get away with it after all.

'SILENCE! One hour detention, all of you,' said the enraged nose. 'Turner, step forward. How do you plead?'

Tommy shuffled nearer to the desk.

'Not guilty, sir,' he gulped.

'WHAT? Speak up, boy.'

'Not guilty, sir,' Tommy squeaked.

'WHAT!'

'Not g—'

'It's true, Mr Hargreeves. It can't have been Tommy, sir. I saw him running up Main Stairs.'

The whole room spun round towards the voice. In the shadows sat Trevor Dogooder, a tiny squirt of a lad, who was squirming about on a chair, his hand raised high in the air. No one had noticed him until now. 'I tried to tell you about those two, Mr Hargreeves, sir, he cried pointing at Tommy and Simon. 'They ran up the stairs while you were putting on your wig—'

Trevor clamped his hand over his mouth but too late; the damage was done. Tommy could feel a snigger bubbling up inside him but managed to gulp it back down before it turned into a snort.

'WHAT!' yelled the Headmaster.

'Nothing, sir.'

'Get out, out, this instant. I'll deal with you later,' bellowed Mr Hargreeves, about to explode. Trevor scurried from the room.

'Main Stairs?' He turned back to Tommy and Simon with tight, angry eyes. 'And what pray tell me what you were doing on Main Stairs?'

Tommy and Simon stood rooted to the spot, while the other gang members stared at the floor, unable to help. Tommy could see the Higgins Twins nudging each other, gloating. *They can't get away with it,* he thought ruefully. *It's not fair—it's just not—*

At last, he managed to find his voice.

'We saw someone shaking out the sneezing powder and went after them, sir. Main Stairs was the quickest way up.'

'And who was this someone?'

'We're not sure, sir,' said Simon glumly. 'We were only trying to help.'

'Help, eh, help? Well, I'll teach you to help. One week's kitchen duty each. That will teach you not to disobey school rules.' He turned to the rest of the boys. 'Empty your pockets now, all of you. I'll soon find out who is the perpetrator of the crime. And woe betide you when I do.'

Tommy glanced around at his mates as he reached slowly into his pockets, trying to recall the objects lurking within: banned conkers,

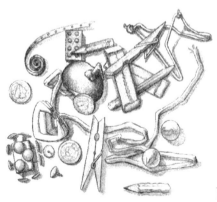

coded messages, all sorts of paraphernalia. Every item a possible reprimand. Why had he not eaten that last piece of chewing gum yesterday? That was bound to be another detention.

Mr Hargreeves scanned each object as it was extracted and placed in separate piles on the desk. Every so often he barked another punishment;

sure enough the gum got two hours extra algebra.

Soon everyone's pockets were empty. Everyone's that is, except Shaun, who stood there with panic rising in his eyes.

Mr Hargreeves turned to him, eyebrows raised.

'HIGGINS,' he roared. 'What is the meaning of this? Do you think you are above the rest of these wrongdoers? Special? Should we be bowing to His Royal Majesty? Ha! You little worm. Empty your pockets now. This instance, I tell you.'

'But there's nothing in them, sir. Honest,' cried Shaun.

'Nothing in them? Nothing in them? I'll give you nothing in them. Matron, if you please,' he beckoned her over to Shaun, 'search his pockets, all of them. Leave nothing to chance. I'll get to the bottom of this if it's the last thing I do.'

First, Matron searched his blazer pockets. Some paperclips, a piece of string, a couple of bits of crumpled paper and a half-sucked boiled sweet were piled on the desk. His trouser pockets showed the same innocent results.

Tommy stood there in panic. *It must have been Shaun*, he thought, *but where is the pepper pot? If he gets away with this, then goodbye life. He'll find a way to kill me, that's for sure.* He thought back to their first encounter. The way the Twins had trapped him. What would they have done if his mum had not turned up? Stolen his money, no question, even though it had been hidden away—hidden away!

'Secret pocket,' gasped Tommy. 'He's got a secret pocket.'

'Take off his blazer, Matron, so we can search it,' ordered Mr Hargreeves.

Matron yanked at the blazer, but Shaun was struggling like a bear caught in a trap.

'Stop it, le'go,' Shaun shouted.

All of a sudden, Matron gave one enormous tug, and off fell the blazer. Out of the lining flew the pepper pot, across the enormous desk and—THUD—straight into Mr Hargreeves's left eye.

'OUCH,' he yelled, hopping around the room, clutching his face.

Shaun swung round and glared at Tommy. 'It was him,' he cried in desperation. 'He must have put it there. I'm innocent.'

But it was too late.

'Got you, you nasty little maggot,' sneered Mr Hargreeves, his eye already beginning to swell. He turned to the others. 'Out. OUT. Out of my sight. Get out now. Higgins and Higgins, stay behind. I believe a telephone call to your parents is in order.'

Tommy breathed a sigh of relief as the gang filed out of Mr Hargreeves' office. That was a close call. It could have easily been *him* left in the room and *his* parents Mr Hargreeves was phoning right now. He could imagine his mother's tight lips, her bristling indignation towards him, her ingratiating smarm towards his headmaster. But that was what it would remain. Imagination. He had been saved. And better still, the Higgins Twins had been caught.

❧ Chapter 22 ❧

A Favour to Ask

Tommy drew to a halt outside Petrovsky's Toy Store, having rushed there as fast as possible after finishing detention and washing a hundred thousand dinner plates. Well, it had seemed that many to him. Just as he and Simon had been leaving the kitchen, they spied Mr and Mrs Higgins pulling up in their Rolls Royce, the result of a large lottery win a couple of years ago, Simon explained, pointing to the personalised number plate 'H1GNS'. Mrs Higgins teetered from the car, a handkerchief pressed to her grief-stricken eyes, and off they hurried to Mr Hargreeves' office to plead the case of their innocent, darling boys.

'Bet they'll offer to re-turf the sports ground, if all else fails,' mumbled Simon.

As Tommy chained up his bike, he could see Mr Petrovsky peering through the shop window. He glanced at his watch—five-thirty. It was already way later than he had promised, and his mind was bubbling like an overheated cauldron—only they were thoughts spilling over the edge, not spells. Why had Mr Petrovsky been so anxious to see him today? What would he tell him? Was he ill? And how long would it take? He had promised his mum he'd be home by six, and he would never make it in time. She was going to be furious with him, especially when he handed her the letter he had been given after all the washing up: the letter explaining why he had been given detention. And if he did not give it to her, somehow lost it in his school bag, she would surely find out at the next parents' evening.

And that would be even worse. She would never let him ride his bike to school again.

Tommy entered the shop, and Mr Petrovsky rushed over, his brow riddled with anxiety. He clasped Tommy's hands and heaved a great sigh of relief.

'Oh, thank goodness you're here. We're safe now. I had started to think you wouldn't turn up, and then where would we have been?'

'Sorry, I got held up at school,' said Tommy, feeling rather guilty. 'What do you mean "safe now"? Has something happened?'

'Come down below. I must talk to you urgently. It's a matter of life and death.' Mr Petrovsky locked the shop door and, after turning over the CLOSED sign, led the way to the basement.

The tea things were already set out in the small office, and a fire was roaring nicely. Mr Petrovsky must have expected him quite a while ago. Tommy plonked himself down on his usual favourite chair and waited while Mr Petrovsky paced around the room. He walked to and fro a few times, wringing his hands, then turned to Tommy.

'Do you remember I told you last time you were here that my mother was murdered?' he started.

Tommy nodded, unsure of what was to come.

'Well, it happened exactly sixty-six years ago today. Sixty-six years since my father and I fled our home. Sixty-six years since I last saw or heard from my grandmother. My *babushka*. All these years I have wondered what became of her. Whether she managed to survive. But it was impossible to find out. Our lives were in grave danger, and it was essential that once we left, we should never again have contact with our past.'

Tommy did not know how to reply. Everything he thought to say seemed silly and insignificant. It was impossible to imagine the terribleness of losing your mother, grandmother and home in a matter of a few hours. Never to be able to return to the only comfort and security you had ever known. What if it ever happened to him? If Sally and his mum and dad suddenly disappeared and he was left alone? No. It was impossible to imagine.

Mr Petrovsky slumped into a chair and continued.

'My father and I were out in the far field when the news came of my mother. I remember seeing my grandmother running across the newly ploughed field, tripping in the furrows. Her boots were heavy with great clods of soil, her skirt billowing in the wind. I waved hello, but she did not return it, and I felt cross she did not react. It was so unlike her. My father stopped work and stood staring. His face frozen. Knowing. I looked at my father and felt his fear. Something terrible had happened.

'When at last she arrived, my father said simply, "Anna?" and my grandmother nodded. My father then said, "Take the boy. Hurry. We need some food and a few clothes, that's all. I'll join you shortly".

'My grandmother hurried me back to the house. She gripped my hand as I stumbled again and again in the furrows. I wanted to tell her it hurt and to stop, but her sense of urgency silenced me. When we got to the house, she said, "Run to the chicken house and hide, *rebenok*. No matter what you see or hear, do not come out. We'll come and fetch you in a while."

'It seemed like hours that I hid in the chicken house. I sat as still as a mouse, peering out through a hole in the side. It started to get dark, and the yard turned grey and then invisible. Every sound or rustle was magnified in the stillness. Each second, I expected to hear heavy boots marching their way up to the house, sweeping my life into oblivion. I had almost given up hope and decided to venture out, when I heard my father's hushed voice calling me in my true name, "Come now, Nikolai. It is time."

'My grandmother was silent as she held me close to her apron, but I could feel the hidden sobs of anguish inside her chest. She held me so tight I thought she would suffocate me in her embrace. I didn't understand why at the time, but she knew it was the last time we would be together.

'We headed for the village, but after walking a short way along the dirt track, my father veered off and cut through the woods. He said the track was too dangerous, and I believed his wild eyes. We followed the path as near to the river as possible, crossing over from time to time in the shallow parts to hide our trail and scent. We had to get downstream towards the village bridge, as it was our only way out; the mountains were too dangerous at that time of year. I still remember the bushes and thorns cutting into my legs as we ploughed on relentlessly through the thick forests. I kept asking my father to stop, but he brushed my pleas away, saying we had not a single second to lose.

'As we neared the outskirts of the village, I saw flashes of red lighting up the dark sky, crackling and dancing as they shot upwards.

The village was on fire. As we drew closer, I could hear the villagers' cries and children's wails mingling with the fire's rage. Terror echoed around the narrow streets. But somehow, we had to get through. We slipped quietly along the smoke clogged passageways, changing course again and again as the fire played cat and mouse with us. People were running through the streets, clutching their few precious belongings. Escaping the onslaught of the inferno. In their terror we were invisible to them, even though they stared through us with grief-stricken eyes.

'We turned a corner and then another. Into the village square. Then we saw them. The MGB, Stalin's Secret Police. They were searching houses, burning them to a cinder, massacring all who stood in their path. Their orders were to find and kill, regardless of what they destroyed on the way. The sight was pure carnage. An unjust battle between power and innocence. Nothing was sacred. My father ran back and forth, desperate to find an escape. But it was useless. We were trapped between them and the fire. I knew if they found us, we would surely be killed without a moment's grace. I looked at my father, hoping to find the answer in his trusted face, but instead I saw utter fear. All was lost. We were alone. Time had come to an end.'

'But what happened?' cried Tommy.

Mr Petrovsky stared at him. It was the same piercing stare Tommy had felt when they first met, his eyes burning into Tommy's soul.

'You. You happened.'

'What!'

'It was you, Tommy. You found us there. You led us out to safety.'

'Me? I did that? How could I have done that?'

'I recognised you the moment I saw you come into the shop. Unforgettable. You saved my life and my father's. I will never know how to repay you.'

The room was swimming. The fire's heat choked Tommy as he tried to understand what was happening. It seemed so unreal, a joke or maybe a mistake, and yet he knew that it was not. Mr Petrovsky was telling the truth.

'Do you understand what this means, Tommy? You have to wear the T-shirt. Tonight. You have to come and save us tonight, or all this will vanish into thin air, will never have existed.'

Tommy could feel the panic rising inside, burning his throat. He was responsible for two lives. It was up to him and him alone to rescue them.

'But what if I can't find you? Or even if I do, how will I know a way out?'

'I don't know. Honestly, I don't know, but somehow you must have found a way because here I am all these years later. Alive because of you and your bravery.'

'The third lesson,' said Tommy quietly.

'The third lesson, yes. Valour. The power to help and protect those around you. Can you do it? Can you help me?'

Tommy looked at the old man—his friend—who had helped him so much. Who had given him the strength and encouragement to find his way at High Brooms. Given him the means to have adventures beyond anyone's imagination. Would this time be the same? Would Tommy feel safe in the knowledge he would return again to his real life, or would it be different? Could he do it? Risk his life to save another? Deep down he already knew the answer. He had to try. Whatever the risk. Whatever the danger. He had to believe in himself and in the greater good of life itself.

'Yes, I'll do it, I'll help you,' he answered at length. 'Of course I will. What else can I do?'

The old man grasped Tommy's hands and, as he held them tight, a sudden warmth burnt into Tommy's fingers, shooting up through his body, giving him the strength to perform the task that lay ahead. It was the same strength he had felt when he had lifted Perseus' sword high into the air.

'Don't worry, Mr Petrovsky. I'll find you, whatever it takes.'

✎ Chapter 23 ✎

A Journey to Russia

It was precisely six-forty-three when Tommy finally arrived home to Parsons Court. He had been right to be worried about his lateness, for it was like voluntarily stepping into a viper's nest when the viper, its whole family and all its friends were lying in wait for your arrival. He had managed to open the front door without being spotted—his plan being to sneak upstairs and pretend he had fallen asleep—but as his right foot landed softly on the bottom step of the staircase, a shriek filled the hallway. Sally!

'Mum!' she yelled, 'he's back. Tommy's back.' She stuck out her tongue and blew a raspberry. Tommy glared at her, then stomped upstairs as Sally went running into the kitchen to fetch their mum.

Tommy slammed his bedroom door and threw himself on his bed. He hated this house. He hated his life. And most of all he hated his stupid sister. Why had she done that to him after all he had done for her that morning?

Now he could hear his mum yelling up the stairs, demanding he come down right now and explain where he had been. Her words were making his head hurt. What had he done that was so wrong? The yelling stopped, but in their place came the firm tread of footsteps on the staircase. Tommy buried his head under his pillow, wishing himself away. Did he have time to put on his T-shirt? Quick. He fumbled under his pillow, where he had left the shirt that morning— like every morning. Where was it? His head was pounding. Where was the T-shirt? He chucked his pillow on the floor and dived under his duvet—nothing. It was gone. The T-shirt was gone.

His bedroom door flew open and there stood his mother, silhouetted in the doorframe.

'TOMMY!'

'WHERE'S MY T-SHIRT? What have you DONE with it?' Tommy threw his duvet on the floor, then lunged after it and started scrambling around under his bed, hunting for the shirt.

'WHAT?' his mum shrieked, staring at her son flailing about like a fish in a desert. She looked rather like a goldfish herself, her mouth silently flapping up and down in disbelief. Tommy spun round and glared at his mum.

'My T-shirt. Where is it? What have you done with it?'

'What? I— I put it in the wash.' His mum shook the muddle out of her head. 'Now, where have you been?'

Tommy's months of frustration erupted into a cacophony of noises that resembled a mishmash of jungle animals fighting over the last few sips of a watering hole. His mum stood staring, gawping in her goldfish-like way, as though she was waiting for her son to start foaming at the mouth. The noise went on and on, bouncing off the walls of his tiny, square bedroom. It did not seem to belong to him. He had no control over what would come out next.

Finally, Tommy thumped his fist on the floor and spat through clenched teeth,

'I was late. So what. Get over it.'

He slumped on the floor and waited for the yelling to start. But instead there was silence. Tommy squeezed his eyes so tight his brain hurt—it was the best way to block out the world. Mr Petrovsky, his friend. He would fail him now for sure.

A firm hand rested on his shoulder, but he kept his eyes tightly shut. Nothing could make it better. Nothing. He could feel his mum sitting down next to him, her arm creeping round his neck. He felt tense, wary, angry—he wanted to roll up into a protective ball like a spikey hedgehog. She gently squeezed his shoulder. Was his mum being nice to him? Is that what nice felt like?

'Tommy?' She hesitated. 'Tommy, what's wrong?'

He shrugged her arm away. He did not want her 'nice'. Too little, too late. He just wanted his T-shirt and to be left alone. For them all to disappear. He turned away; back hunched, arms folded, eyes tight. Visions of Mr Petrovsky kept flashing into his head. Tramping through the woods. Tripping on the tree roots. Heading towards his death.

The room stayed silent for what seemed like forever. Then he felt his mum plant a tiny kiss on the top of his head and rise to her feet. At the doorway, she hesitated, 'I'll leave some shepherd's pie in the oven, in case you're hungry later,' she said. Then she turned and left.

Tommy stayed motionless on the floor. He could have turned into one of Medusa's statues for all he cared. He did not want to get up. He did not want to start again. Why did life always go wrong, just when it seemed to be going right?

His brain jumped. A noise. Footsteps creeping into his room and stopping just in front of him. He waited, silently; praying whoever it was would just go away.

'Tommy.'

Sally. It was Sally. How dare she come in and gloat at him. He felt a hot lump of hate rise in his throat.

'Tommy.' She poked his arm. 'Tommy, wake up.' A low snarl escaped through his nose. Why was she always so horrible to him? Why did she always tell on him? His eyes flicked open: hatred flooding out of them like two laser-gun beams.

'Why did you tell on me?' The words tasted as bitter as a Brussels sprout.

'Sorry, Tommy. I'm sorry.' She dropped something into his lap. 'I found your T-shirt.' A hot tear ran down Sally's face.

'Why do you always hate me? What have I ever done to you?' Tommy's mouth felt funny, all twisty and gnarled.

'I don't hate you, I don't. It's just—' Sally hesitated, '—it's just— it's not fair.' She sank to the floor next to Tommy.

'What's not fair?'

'You. You have everything.'

171

'Me?' Tommy sneered. 'Me? You think I have everything? That's ridiculous! It's you. It's you, Sally, who has everything. My whole life revolves around "what Sally wants". Stupid dolls, constant treats, Mum. You have everything single, little thing you could ever possibly want in the whole of your sad, pathetic life.'

'Except freedom. You can go wherever you want, do whatever you want. I can't even go outside unless Mum's there. You think I want to be treated like a baby every second of every day?'

'You do a good job pretending, if you don't!' huffed Tommy, not wanting to hear her excuses. He shot another laser look at Sally. 'Go play with your stupid Barbie or whatever, just get out of my room.'

Tommy sat there wrapped in his sadness for a good while longer after Sally had left. His sorrow was like a cloak of steel pinning him to the floor, making his head feel all cloggy and full of cotton wool. But right in the centre of all the stuffiness lay a pinprick of thought—like a sharp intense vibration. It felt hot and throbby, and with every breath it grew larger and louder, piercing his grim-reaper's gloom.

His eyes flicked open. The room was full of dusky shadows but there in his lap lay the T-shirt: glowing, positively humming with electricity. Now. Now was the time. The time to go and rescue Mr Petrovsky.

✳

All was still in Parsons Court. The wind lapped gently around the solid brick houses. Now and again it whipped up a dancing leaf that waltzed off down the road before settling back to sleep. Most of the rooms were already in darkness, their occupants dreaming about lazy summer holidays, waking up to a magically cleaned house, or winning the lottery. The ten o'clock news flickered in the downstairs windows as the newsreader announced the day's events to an already snoring audience. It was the end of an exhausting week. Peace and calm reigned in the safe, suburban cul-de-sac.

Upstairs in his tiny square bedroom, Tommy lay staring at the ceiling. He had been staring at it for the last hour and a half, with only a bluebottle to keep him company. He had tried counting sheep, reading by torchlight and hitting his head five times on the pillow. But no matter what he tried, his eyes stayed stubbornly open. And he just had to get to sleep right now. Mr Petrovsky and his father could be running through the burning village this very minute, and where was Tommy? In bed. Awake.

He got out of bed and walked across to the window. There was Mr Brown's Doberman, Fred, taking his owner for their usual 'do your business before bedtime' walk. Mr Brown's short stubby legs whirled like a hamster's on a wheel as he tried to keep up.

Tommy looked up toward the clear round moon; it was just a chink away from its fullness. Beyond, the many thousand stars and planets twinkled their existence to the world below. Somewhere up there, in the far reaches of the universe, lay Yorintown and the Anjulongs.

I've been up there, he thought. *I've sailed the solar system and seen lands that no one else in this lifetime will ever know exist.* The thought made him realise for the first time in his life just how minuscule he was in comparison to time itself. A mere speck in the continual wheel of existence. And yet at this very moment in history the significance of his life was about to be tested. His actions would have an everlasting effect on the lives of Mr Petrovsky and his father, and who knew how many other innocent people. *There is so much out there I shall never know about, and yet it exists, as I do, waiting to be discovered.*

Tommy looked at the stars twinkling back their agreement. He realised that most of them had looked upon Earth since the day it was born. That they had witnessed the terrible evil humans were capable of inflicting on each other but also knew of the goodness that existed within most of the inhabitants. Many years ago, they had twinkled over the little village in the foothills of the Ural Mountains and had helped a boy—him—along on his adventure. *Please help me now,* he whispered, *help me get started on my journey.*

A soft breeze blew gently though the tiny square bedroom. Tommy felt it tingling his spine and shivered. He looked once again at the night sky and then slipped quietly off the windowsill and into bed. As he snuggled up into the warmth of his duvet, he felt a prickle of excitement rushing through his body.

I'm coming, Mr Petrovsky, he whispered sleepily. *Just hold on, I'm on my way.*

*

A second before he hit the water, Tommy woke up. He was plummeting through the air, down, down, down, no way to stop, and then—*SMASH*—he plunged into the icy depths. Water gushed over his head. It bubbled and frothed with rage as it pulled him further and further towards the riverbed below. He fought hard, conscious of only one thing. *I must get to the surface. I must breathe.*

But the water was strong. It squeezed the air from his chest, stung his ears, burning into his lungs as he was tossed from rock to rock. Over and over he tumbled, crashing, scraping, dragging, drowning. With his remaining strength, Tommy pushed against the current, his arms slicing through the water. Suddenly, his head broke the surface and the cold evening air came rushing into his lungs.

But the current was still thrusting him along, threatening to take him under again, ramming him against the rough rocks. It was like a stalking cat. Patting and playing, preparing for its kill. And Tommy, the mouse, was trapped and terrified. He fought against the river's pull, until finally he was able to grab hold of an overhanging branch and drag himself out onto the muddy bank.

He lay there shivering with cold, unconscious of anything but his pounding heart and throbbing head. A rough cotton shirt and heavy work trousers clung like glue to his wet body. When his breathing had stilled, he unclenched his fist and stared at the small flask. He had held on to it so tightly as he fell asleep, praying he could bring it with him. He breathed a sigh of relief. It had not been lost in the river, washed away into oblivion. He needed the flask and its contents. It was his safety net. His 'just in case'.

Tommy sat up and took in his surroundings. He was sitting in a wide gorge, cut in two by a deep, narrow river rushing down from the distant mountains. Looming high above him lay dark, gloomy forests. There was no way he could climb up to them; it was much too steep and rocky. *Not that I really want to*, he thought, gulping at the idea of wolves and bears waiting to pounce as he reached the top. What he had to do was get dry and warm, but he had no idea how to start a fire. He wrung some water out of his shirt. *I have no clue where I am, what I'm going to do, or how on earth I shall find Mr Petrovsky*, he thought, as a great warm tear welled up in his eye.

Way above Tommy's head, the evening sky was settling down to sleep. Soon it would be dark and night creatures would be prowling. Wet and cold and very much alone in the middle of nowhere, Tommy felt about as much an adventurer as a piece of toast. And he could have sat there all night feeling sorry for himself, but there was too much to do. Tommy had arrived here, wherever 'here' was, for a purpose. To save Mr Petrovsky and become a hero. He had to get moving, find civilisation and find his friend.

Reluctantly, Tommy hauled himself to his feet and trudged off downstream, his sodden boots squelching like a bog with every step. The riverbank was slippery and steep and littered with outcrops of rocks protruding over the water's edge.

He was picking his way across an extra-large boulder when he first sensed the danger creeping beside him; its footsteps were as soft as a tiptoeing ghost. He paused, afraid to turn around, his heightened senses scanning his surroundings. A deathly silence answered him. He picked up his pace again, telling himself it was just his imagination but a few metres further and fear buzzed in his head. Had that not been the faintest sound of a twig snapping?

But again, the night sent back silence. Nothing. Tommy was alone. *Yes, that's right I'm alone*, he told himself, a shiver of cold and wet and unease trying to persuade him otherwise.

And it was right to do so, for a noise pierced the evening calm. A loud fearful hiss. He swung round and saw perched on a rock above him a large cat. Its eyes glistened in the semi-darkness. Its mouth curled into a razor-sharp snarl. The lynx spat again, then sprang high into the air, its claws ready to cut through Tommy's back. He leapt away and grabbed hold of a large branch that had been caught in the river rocks. The cat landed nimbly on its feet, coiled back, then sprung again.

Tommy swung the branch, knocking the cat away. It whipped round, hissing and spitting, and leapt for Tommy's throat. Again, he tried to beat it back, but the cat lashed out, striking Tommy's shoulder with its claws and ripping through his shirt. Tommy dodged to the right as the beast's claws grazed his flesh beneath. Suddenly, he remembered the grip of Perseus' mighty sword. Its power rocketed through his body like an exploding firework. He swung the branch over his head and brought it crashing down on top of the lynx. The animal howled in agony and slumped to the floor, dazed but not dead.

Gasping for breath, Tommy dropped the branch and stared at the cat, shuddering at the sight of its Dracula fangs protruded from its limp mouth. His heart was pounding like a bass speaker on full volume. What a near miss! One millimetre more, and his shoulder would have been mincemeat. Him as well, most probably. The lynx twitched a paw. It was stirring. Time to get going. Tommy picked the branch off the ground—no way was he leaving his makeshift sword behind—and taking one last deep breath, resumed his journey onwards.

On and on Tommy trudged. The sky had darkened by now, and one by one the stars flickered their nightly welcome, bringing some relief to the greyness ahead. He still felt miserable, but at least he was a little warmer with all the marching and climbing. A little further, and Tommy looked up and saw the forest had thinned and the sky ahead was streaked with an orange glow. *I must be nearing the village*, he thought, quickening his pace in relief.

As he got closer, he could see the glow flickering and twirling, dancing an endless tarantella above the silhouetted rooftops. He reached the outskirts of the village with still no way out of the gorge. Cracking, hissing, snapping sounds punctured the night air. The stench of sulphur invaded his nostrils. Fire. The village was on fire. Way above him, orange flames leapt into the night, engulfing all in sight. The river had narrowed by now, the rocks giving way to sheer walls. Any hope of climbing up had vanished, and Tommy prayed he would soon find a set of stairs or a ladder to help him out.

Above him a rickety wooden bridge spanned the river, marking the only route from the village and the treacherous mountains beyond. *If I ever find Mr Petrovsky, then we must cross this bridge. It's our only chance,* he reasoned, thankful he had found their escape.

A coarse laugh broke into his thoughts. Standing on the bridge were half a dozen uniformed men, laughing and talking in low, gruff voices. Tommy's hopes sank as quickly as they had risen. How would they get past the guards? Even if he found Mr Petrovsky, they would be trapped in the burning village. One of the soldiers flicked a cigarette butt over the bridge and watched it fall into the river below. Fearful they would see him, Tommy drew back silently into the shadows and, as he did, saw ahead of him an opening in the wall. A way up perhaps? He groped his way as silently as possible towards the gap until he was upon it. The hole looked bigger from here, large enough for him to climb up into, and perhaps it was his only chance to reach the village square. Without a moment's thought, Tommy hauled himself up and plunged into the dark passageway.

It was damp and pitch-black inside, blacker than anything Tommy had ever known before. Water sloshed into his boots as he waded through long-trapped floodwater. It smelt as though life itself had ended in here: rotten, mildewed, stagnant. He tried not to breathe it in but had no choice. He had to keep going.

Blindly, he fumbled his way along, bent half double by the low ceiling, imagining eerie eyes staring at him through the blackness. He was exhausted, frightened, wet and despondent, but one thought kept him pushing forward. Mr Petrovsky.

On and on Tommy plodded until finally he saw ahead of him a thin, straight shaft of dim light falling from the ceiling—light from the burning village. Hope leapt into his heart. A way up. He splashed through the water towards it, nearly tumbling into a small, circular pit as he reached the end of the tunnel. He had found a well, with its smooth round walls rising towards freedom and its endlessness disappearing into the darkness below. He was perched about halfway up on a roughly hewn ledge, and—there! A ladder. If he could just reach it. He caught hold of the edge of the rocks with one hand and stretched with all his might towards the ladder. His fingers found the edge of the rusty steps, and grabbing hold, he swung himself over.

The ladder was slippery and corroded in places, grazing his hands as he gripped it. Up, up, up. He neared the top, hearing screams and shouts echoing above him. Thick black clouds of deadly smoke hung in the air, blocking any view of the sky beyond. He was in the village square. He had made it!

Tommy reached the top and peered over the side of the well. Villagers were running from all directions. Mothers yelling for their children, their terrified faces lit up by dancing flames. Babies crying. Young, old and weak scattering throughout the village square, trying to escape the carnage. He saw the grey raincoats of the soldiers, the insignia of the MGB stamped firmly on their sleeves. Torches, guns. Flames engulfing the wooden houses. Bodies lying deathly still on the ground.

He raced through the square, hunting this way and that for Mr Petrovsky. Staring into horror-stricken faces that stared blindly back at him.

Someone banged into him, causing him to stumble forward. He spun round. A woman, her haunting eyes searing into his soul. Her hand clenching the little girl's arm beside her. Blonde hair, tear-stained eyes. It could have been Sally. Mum and Sally. The realisation punched through Tommy's heart like a prize-fighter's right hook. A mother protecting her child. He thought about his mum, her possessiveness over his sister and how much it hurt him. And in that split second, deep down, in the tiniest segment right at the bottom of his heart, he understood why. She blamed herself for Sally's epilepsy.

The woman brushed past, her only purpose being to find safety for her child. He watched them vanish into the crowds. Onwards. Forwards. He had to move forwards. He had to help his mum find the love he knew she had for him. And he would, yes, he would. But first he had to find Mr Petrovsky.

Where was he? Where was he? He must be here. There. A boy standing alone. He dashed over and swung him round.

There was no mistaking those piercing blue eyes. Eyes full of fear and horror and tears.

'It's me, I've found you,' Tommy cried, grabbing hold of the boy. The boy flinched away, panic spreading through his face.

'Mr Petrovsky—Nicolas—I've come to get you. I know a way out.'

But the boy remained motionless, stuck in a bubble of fear. A heavy hand clasped Tommy's shoulder, and he veered round, staring into eyes the same blue as the boy's. Mr Petrovsky's father—it must be him.

'Come with me, please come with me. I can help you,' pleaded Tommy, his desperation clear to see; he had to get them out of there, right away. The man grabbed Tommy's arm and leant towards him, defeat welling in his eyes.

'Over,' he said, his voice barely audible above the madness surrounding them.

'But I know a way out through the well,' begged Tommy, pointing towards the middle of the square. 'I came from there. It's safe. I have to help you. Please come with me, please. We need to get to the well.'

'Well?'

'The well, yes.' Hope poured into Tommy's heart. 'There's a passage halfway down that leads to the river. We can make it, please hurry. We must go now.' He took a couple of steps, then turned back and beckoned for them to follow. 'Come on.'

The man nodded and gripped his son's trembling hand. 'Come, Nikolai.' He turned back to Tommy, 'You—I trust.'

Tommy ran back through the square. Behind him, the father had picked up his scared son and was running with all his might, away from the horror, towards their safety.

They reached the edge of the well, and Tommy turned to the man.

'I'll go first. I know the way,' he said and clambered swiftly over the edge. He could hear the man coxing his son to follow and reached out a hand to help the younger boy over the side of the well. As soon as he was safely on the other side, the older man scrambled in behind him and together they set off down the rusty ladder.

They descended into the darkness below, the cries of the villagers fading into the distance as they were swallowed by the steepness of the walls. The ladder creaked and groaned with each step, complaining at this sudden invasion after all these years of peace, but thankfully, it held strong, and at last they reached the passageway. Tommy felt so tired he could barely lift one foot after the other. He did not know if he could go on, but he knew he must. There was no other way. Through the passageway they stumbled in silence, broken only by the splashing of water and their laboured breathing.

When it had long seemed as though the tunnel would never end, Tommy realised they had reached its mouth. He turned back to the others, holding his finger to his mouth to indicate silence, and then peered out of the opening, towards the bridge. Above him, the place was swarming with dozens of soldiers. Any thought of escape over the bridge vanished with this first glance. There was no way they could risk climbing up onto the bridge or even swimming over to the other side; it would be suicide. In the darkness, Tommy could just make out two large trucks, their engines ticking over, as the soldiers herded countless women and children into the back of them. As he watched silently, a scuffle broke out amongst the prisoners as the soldiers jostled them towards the trucks, and the other soldiers, who had been guarding the bridge, moved in to break up the chaos. This was their one chance.

'Quick, follow me. Quietly now.'

He hastened out of the tunnel, keeping as close to the wall as possible so he was hidden amongst the shadows, and led them swiftly along the edge of the riverbank. Above them, he could hear the shouts and cries of the frightened prisoners and the gruff harsh voices of the soldiers, trying to keep control.

There was no choice but to retrace his steps along the river until they could find a place to cross it. It was impossible; exhaustion was turning his mind delirious. How would they ever reach safety? Still they kept going, keeping close to the cliffs, hiding in the night shadows, until at last they were out of the village.

As the last light from the burning village faded into the distance, Tommy knew he had to rest. He had not one ounce of energy left, not one step more to keep him on his way. He felt dizzy and sick with fever, and his arm was burning again from the lynx attack, even though it seemed a million years ago. He turned to the others, motioning to them to stop, and collapsed into a heap on the rocks. The man bent down, his brow riddled with worry, and looked into Tommy's eyes.

'Can we rest for a bit?' Tommy asked.

The man shook his head.

'No stop. Must go on. My son.'

But Tommy knew there was nothing left in him; he would only hinder them if he tried to walk further. His head was pounding with exhaustion; his legs were like iron weights, too heavy even to lift.

'I can't go further. You must go on without me,' he muttered weakly.

'No,' replied the man anxiously.

Tommy hesitated. He did not want to be left alone in the middle of nowhere, but he had done his task. He had led them to safety. Now it was time to say goodbye.

'You must go,' he said at last. 'I shall be safe. I know my way home. Please go!'

The man thought for a moment, unsure of what to do. Then he reached into one of the bundles he had tied around his waist, pulled out a bright object and placed it in Tommy's hand. He looked once more at this stranger who had risked his life to rescue them, then turned to his son.

'Come, Nikolai. We go now.'

The boy rose wearily to his feet, took a few steps towards Tommy and knelt before him. He gently touched his arm, his blue eyes again piercing into Tommy's heart. The words they spoke needed no sound to be understood; the gratitude flowing from them was plain to see.

Then he took his father's hand, and together they walked off into the distance.

Tommy sat silent for a moment, listening to the night sounds of the riverbank. The object glinted in his palm, even in the dim light. It was a huge sapphire. As big as the jewels he had once seen in the Tower of London. It was truly magnificent.

With the little strength he had left, Tommy reached into his pocket and took out the flask he had so carefully held on to. His adventure was over, his task fulfilled. Now it was time to go home. He thought about his tiny, square bedroom and cosy, warm bed waiting so invitingly for him, and he thought he would never again be so happy to see them than he was at that very moment.

Tomorrow, as soon as I wake up, I'll go and see Mr Petrovsky, he thought, taking a sip from the flask. *And afterwards, I'll ask Mum if I can take Sally out on her bike. But right now, I just want to go home.*

Tommy Turner's Tremendous Travels

❧ Chapter 24 ❧

A New Beginning

When Tommy next opened his eyes, he found he was back at home in his tiny, square bedroom in Parsons Court. He felt as though he had slept for a hundred years; his body was so limp and heavy it could have been made from a huge sack of potatoes. He lay there for a moment, staring up at the ceiling, remembering last night's events. But it was over now, and he was safe. And he had saved the lives of Mr Petrovsky and his father.

The sapphire lay grasped in his hand. Tommy examined it in wonderment. In the night-time, it had looked magnificent, but now in the daylight, its beauty was beyond description. He thought for a moment more, undecided about what to do. When he had made up his mind, he got out of bed and began the day.

After he had dressed, he put his flask carefully back in the box Mr Petrovsky had given him for his treasures. Then he put the sapphire in his pocket and went downstairs for breakfast.

Sally and his mum were already busy in the kitchen. Tommy hovered by the door, unsure what to say or what to do. His cheeks felt hot and red, and he realised he was rather ashamed about his behaviour the evening before. It made him feel a bit sick inside, like he had just eaten a massive chocolate bar all in one go.

His mum turned around, her hands full with a big platter of sausages, bacon and scrambled egg, and jumped at the sight of Tommy loitering by the door.

'Come in—Tommy—love,' she stuttered, her eyes looking anywhere but at him. 'Come and have some breakfast; it's your favourite.' She dashed to the table, head down. Tommy shuffled a bit closer. Why was Mum acting weird?

She glanced at Sally and then again at him.

'We made it specially, didn't we, Sally?' Sally nodded and looked sheepishly at her brother. 'Come on, sit yourself down,' continued his mum, spooning an extra piece of bacon onto his plate. 'You must be starving.' Tommy plonked himself at the table. He did not want to admit it, but he had a hole the size of the Grand Canyon in his tummy, and those sausages looked as though they would fit perfectly.

He squinted at his mum, and their eyes, meeting for a brief, awkward moment, spoke the words that neither mum nor son could say to each other. *It will all be okay. We will all be okay.* Then his mum turned away and started cutting up the food on Sally's plate.

"Stop it, I can do it.' Sally pushed her plate out of her mum's reach. 'Please, Mum, stop treating me like I'm three years old.' She sliced a piece of sausage and stuck it in her mouth.

'Oh. I see.' Mum stood rooted, mid-slice, for a moment; then she took a long deep breath and sat herself down between the two of them.

Tommy glanced surreptitiously at his mum, then he glanced at Sally. And then his eye did a funny thing—it winked at Sally. Then Sally's eye winked back at him. And then, before they knew it, they were both sharing a rather small but nevertheless rather significant secret brother-sister grin. And then Tommy went back to eating his sausages.

*

Mr Petrovsky was busy sorting out a Halloween display when Tommy arrived at the shop. He looked up and hurried over to greet him.

'Oh, you're safe, thank goodness! I have been so worried. Come downstairs, come downstairs and tell me all.' He called to Simon, his Saturday boy, to mind the shop, and the two friends hurried down to the basement.

'Let me look at you. Are you fine? Are you hurt?' asked Mr Petrovsky as soon as they entered the office.

'A bit tired, I suppose. Apart from that, just the scratch from my fight with the lynx, and that's not as bad as I first thought,' said Tommy, unconsciously touching his arm.

'A lynx? My goodness. You did have an adventure last night, and now you must tell me all about it.'

When the two had finished their stories, Tommy reached into his pocket, took out the sapphire and handed it to the old man.

'Mr Petrovsky, I think this is rightfully yours. Your father gave it to me last night, I mean, all those years ago just before we said goodbye.'

Mr Petrovsky took the gem in his hands, remembering back to that night so many years ago. He looked up at Tommy, the boy who had saved him when he was just a child. Now he was an old man, nearly at the end of his long life.

'It's because of you, Tommy, that I've been blessed with so much happiness,' he said and handed the sapphire back.

'This is yours and justly so, for you are the bravest boy I have ever had the pleasure of knowing. But keep it a secret, just you and me, for it is a great treasure from the days of the Russian Tsars.'

Mr Petrovsky stood up.

'I think I had better be getting back upstairs, or my customers will think I have deserted them,' he laughed. 'Now promise me you will come back soon and let me know what you've been up to.'

'You bet, Mr Petrovsky,' said Tommy, 'and thank you for everything.'

'No, you are the one that needs to be thanked. If it wasn't for you, none of this would have happened.'

*

As Tommy cycled back home to his bedroom, he thought about the last week of his life. Mr Petrovsky, the Anjulongs, Peeves-Withers, and the flask. His adventure with Perseus and flight to safety on Pegasus. He thought about Simon and the Pioneers and wondered what had happened to the Higgins Twins.

Well, that can wait until Monday, he thought, a fizz of excitement bubbling up inside him. Monday afternoon was the first football match of the term. The first football match when he, Tommy Turner, would be captain.

I wonder what will happen next, he thought as he turned into the driveway of his new house in Parsons Court.

Learn to use the Pigpen code

The Pigpen code is simple code that uses symbols instead of letters. An example using tic-tac-toe and X grids is shown below but you can make up any variation with your friends. Just remember you need a different symbol for each letter of the alphabet. Once you and your friends have written out and learnt the code the way you want it, you will all be able to communicate in code.

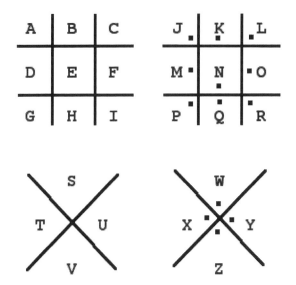

This is how you would write the individual letters if you used the example shown on the previous page:

This is how Tommy writes his name:

>⊡⊐⊐≪ ><⌐⊡□⌐

Printed in Great Britain
by Amazon